THE ANSWER'S LOVE

David Canford

COPYRIGHT © 2023 David Canford

11.24

All rights reserved. No part of this publication may be reproduced, distributed, or transmitted in any form or by any means, or stored in a database or retrieval system, without the prior written permission of the author.

This novel is a work of fiction and a product of the author's imagination. Any resemblance to anyone living or dead (save for named historical figures) or any entity or legal person is purely coincidental and unintended.

CHAPTER 1

The knock on the door was soft, almost inaudible.
"Come on in," called Mosa, wondering who it could possibly be that would knock so diffidently.
The visitor wore a cloak with the hood over her head as if she didn't want to be recognized. The candlelight was weak but strong enough to reveal a young woman's face. She removed her hood and shook her golden locks.
Mosa's stood up from her chair. Her mouth opened in surprise but she was temporarily lost for words. Other than policemen coming to make arrests, Mosa had never before seen a white person in Tremé.
"Hello, I'm Emily."
"I can see who you are. What are you doing here?"
"I'm sorry to just turn up like this but I wanted to apologize."
"There's no need for that. You coming to court saved my son and I'm very grateful."
"Yes but I got him into trouble in the first place by going below deck to talk to him. Is Thomas here?"
"No, he's out but I'll be sure to pass on the message.

It was good of you to come." Mosa moved forward, hoping to encourage Emily to leave. Nothing good could come of her being here. Her innocent sweetness counted for nothing in this world of prejudice. She might have been followed. White folks would be mad as could be that one of their own had come into New Orlean's black faubourg to visit her son. But it wouldn't be Emily who suffered the consequences of their anger.

The door suddenly swung open. Mosa braced herself, fearing Emily's father must have tracked her down.

Emily smiled. "Thomas!"

"Emily? What are you doing here?" Thomas grinned with delight at seeing her.

"She's just leaving." Mosa's voice was terse. "She came to apologize for what you went through. I told her there was no need."

"Exactly," said Thomas. "May I escort you back?"

"Thomas, think," interrupted Mosa. "If anyone sees you two together, they'll get the wrong idea."

"I'll only take Emily as far as Congo Square and see she gets a cab."

Before Mosa could protest further, Thomas placed a hand on Emily's back and gently guided her to the door. Mosa watched in despair. For a black man to touch a white woman was inviting deathly retribution. His acquittal appeared to have given him a misplaced sense of invulnerability.

After they'd left Mosa paced the floor, wringing her hands. Thomas had only just avoided a hanging and now he was risking a lynching were he to be seen in the company of Emily.

The night was unusually humid for the early time of year. At first, Thomas wasn't sure if he was sweating so much from the heat or because of Emily. His fast beating heart told him it must be the latter. "You didn't need to come, you saved me from the noose. You were so brave to appear in court." Thomas turned to look at her but it was a moonless night. The shadows were deep and dark and he couldn't see anything save for the contours of her face.

"I had to, you were innocent."

"You said your attacker was white. Do you know who it was?"

"No, I didn't get a proper look at him. Though I remember he smelled of eau de cologne and whiskey. Anyway, I don't want to talk about that night. It's something I'm trying to forget. Did you get your job back?"

"No, there's no chance of that but I get to play at clubs in the French Quarter some nights, and by day I work down at the port."

Emily tripped on the uneven ground. Without thinking, Thomas grabbed her around the waist, but she quickly pulled away.

"Is that Congo Square? I'll be fine from here." Street lamps ahead beckoned, calling them out of the pitch blackness that was Tremé.

On the other side of the square a horse and

carriage stood, waiting for a fare. Thomas knew he shouldn't but he couldn't help himself. "Did you want to come watch me play?"

"I'm not old enough to get into those kind of places."

"They don't check nobody. And plenty of white folks come to watch, you wouldn't stand out. It's Mardi Gras soon. People will be in costumes, many wear masks. No one need ever know who you are."

"I'm not sure. As you can imagine, I wasn't supposed to be out tonight. My parents think I'm in bed, asleep. I really must go, goodnight."

Thomas remained rooted to the spot after she'd gone, his insides churning.

Outlined by the candlelight from inside, Mosa was waiting by the door, arms akimbo, when Thomas returned.

"Have you lost your mind? Don't you listen to a thing I tell you?"

"I ain't done nuthin'."

"That don't matter. If a white person thinks you have, you're guilty. Miracles don't happen twice. You were lucky once, you won't be again. Promise me you'll stay well away from that girl. She may be sweet and pretty and all but that makes her doubly dangerous." Thomas gave his mother a surly look. "Promise me," she insisted.

Thomas grunted and went to his room.

He struggled to sleep. Emily was in his head and wouldn't leave.

CHAPTER 2

A few days later when there was another gentle knock at the door, Mosa sighed with irritation. Surely it couldn't be that girl again. What on earth was she thinking? She might be young but she couldn't not know how things were in the South.

Mosa exhaled with relief when Lowenna entered.

"I'm sure glad to see you. How's it going? Come and sit down."

"I'm quitting," said Lowenna as she settled into the high backed wooden dining chair next to her friend.

"Well, my offer still stands. You're welcome to live here until you decide what you want to do."

"Thank you but I already know what I'm doing. I'm returning to England."

"England." Mosa repeated in surprise. "I'm sure gonna miss you. We've been friends a long time."

"I'll miss you too but I made a mistake coming back to America, following a son who doesn't want me." Mosa stretched out a hand in sympathy and took hold of Lowenna's. "I'm so sorry." A tinge of guilt ran through Mosa. A true friend would have advised her to stay in England, knowing what Abraham was like and given that he'd never asked his mother to come to New Orleans, but Mosa hadn't had the heart to say that back then. If only she'd had the courage to be frank with her, Lowenna would have remained in England, probably be happily married, and wouldn't have had to sell herself to pay her son's debts.

"There's no need to be sorry. I've made peace with my fate, fighting it won't bring happiness. Abe is never going to talk to me, and I have a past here I can't shake off. Recently I've been feeling homesick, and I've never got used to the stifling heat, it's so draining."

The friends sat chatting long into the evening. When Lowenna left, Mosa hugged her tightly and made her promise faithfully to write this time. She watched her merge with the night, wondering what work her friend would be able to get. It wasn't easy for a single woman to survive, especially at their age. The few doors of opportunity open to them were already closing. A mindless job in a factory and living in squalid accommodation was likely to be Lowenna's life. Mosa was grateful she had teaching to fall back on, there'd always be a demand for that and age wasn't an issue. Schools preferred those with years of experience.

That night Mosa lay awake, unable to sleep and thinking. Homesick, Lowenna had said. Mosa too missed home. The plantation in South Carolina.

The fragrance of jasmine, the birdsong, the croaking of the bullfrogs, and the morning dew like pearls on blades of grass.

She thought about how different her life could have been if she hadn't lost it. A school for the local children. A life of peace and tranquility out of harm's way. The kind of life she'd always wanted but which had always eluded her.

Stop, she reprimanded herself. Thinking like that does nothing but bring a person down. New Orleans, vibrant yet unforgiving, enticing yet threatening, was her home now. It was where her two children were. Mosa turned over and tried to clear her mind so sleep would come. A rooster had already broken the stillness when she finally drifted off.

Emily never did turn up at the club during Mardi Gras. Thomas ventured down to the edge of the Garden District where she lived. Leafy streets and grand houses stretched before him, tempting him, calling him to walk among them and look for her. But there was an invisible barrier for those of his color. If he crossed it, someone would report him. The police would immediately assume his intent was nefarious and he'd be arrested and accused of some crime. For people of his color, an accusation would result in a conviction in all but the rarest of cases.

Agitated and frustrated, Thomas made his way back across town. He thought about taking a streetcar but the one that passed him pulled by a horse and which stopped only feet away didn't have a black star on it. You had to be white to ride a streetcar without a black star.

"Hey, Thomas!" Thomas peered out from his inner world of resentment to see Samuel, the lawyer who had defended him. His tall, wiry figure cast a shadow over Thomas. "How are you doing, man?"

"Good, I guess, and you?"

"I'm planning a protest. I'm intending to take one of the streetcars we ain't supposed to ride, or rather find somebody who will so I can represent them when they get arrested. I'll be arguing segregation is unconstitutional. As you've experienced, the courts of Louisiana are most unlikely to be concerned about that. The case should go all the way to the Supreme Court in Washington where I hope to get a more sympathetic hearing."

Thomas was impressed by Samuel's ambition and saw an opportunity to make his mark, a chance to take a stand. "I'd be happy to be that person you need to ride the streetcar."

"That's mighty good of you but your Mama wouldn't want to see you arrested and kept in prison while the case makes its slow journey to the highest court in the nation, not after what you've recently gone through. And I owe her. If she hadn't taught me for free all those years ago, I'd never have gotten this far. Be sure to give her my regards." Samuel raised a hand in a brief wave and walked on.

Thomas watched him go, annoyed he was being treated like a child. He was a man now, capable of making his own decisions. He didn't need his mother's approval or that of anyone else. He was held back by unseen chains, but chains nonetheless, unable to live life as he wanted. The Constitution might preach that all men were created equal, but despite the abolition of slavery you only had real freedom if your skin was the right color. Thomas wasn't free to live wherever he wanted, or go where he wanted, or fall in love with whoever he wanted. A step out of line and he'd be thrown in jail or left swinging from a tree.

The wealthy were hungry for cheap labor to replace the slaves upon whose backs they'd become extremely rich. Convicts were 'leased' out to work for nothing. Slavery still existed, it was just more subtle than before.

Black people were kept under control and out of power not only by ensuring they couldn't vote, but by incarcerating countless thousands for breaking laws introduced to ensure they remained in poverty. Their sweat and toil upheld an economy to benefit the white population, exactly like it had before the Civil War.

That night, Thomas played at his usual club. Blowing his trumpet usually set him free, taking him to a place where only the music mattered, raising his spirits and chasing the blues away.

Being part of a band and creating a sound that made people smile and dance was the best of feelings.

Tonight, though, even the heady mix of perfume, alcohol, and a joyful, carefree beat didn't release him.

During a break and in need of some alone time, Thomas went out the back door and into the alley. Smoking a cigarette, he watched a big yellow moon take center stage while ghostly clouds drifted by. It reminded him of his time on the Mississippi, the almost imperceptible sound of the restless river, and moonlight shimmering on the water. A time of hope and excitement.

"Hey, nigger!" The gruff voice startled him.

CHAPTER 3

Mosa and Angelique were watching the same moon while seated on the uneven wooden veranda in front of Angelique's one room shack. Close to the Backswamp, the natural noises of the night were loud but calming.

Angelique sighed, a happy sigh. "Nights like this make me think of Africa. What it must be like and where in Africa my ancestors came from. I'd love to go see it one day, wouldn't you?"

"Not really, it's not where I'm from, unless you count a great great grandfather who accounts for the color I am. I came from a white mother and white father."

The revelation silenced Angelique for a moment. "Oh my, I never knew.

"It's not something I talk about often."

"Do your kids know?"

"Not exactly. They can see like everyone else can that I've got some white blood in me. They know that I was a slave, and I've told them I never knew who my parents were. I haven't ever told them I did eventually discover their identity, albeit they disowned me the day I was born so they didn't feel like real parents."

"Do you plan on telling them?"

"I'm not sure. I don't want to undermine their sense of identity. Life is tough enough without that. Believe me, I know. Anyway, Maisie's too young and Thomas is finding it hard to navigate his path in the world. That Emily came to visit a short while ago. Thomas clearly likes her and resents they can't have a relationship. If I told him his maternal grandparents were both white, I think it might push him over the edge, make him reckless, and he'd go do something stupid."

Angelique slowly nodded her head while she listened. "I can see where you're coming from. If only we women ruled the world, I'm sure there wouldn't be all this hatred and division."

"You're sure right," agreed Mosa. "Men are like animals, all fighting to be dominant, the alpha male, and they don't give a damn who suffers as a result."

Thomas turned toward the voice. The man's face was clear enough in the moonlight. Abraham, Lowenna's son. In his right hand he held a bottle, a broken bottle.

"Thought you'd got away with it, didn't you! You should've hung." He advanced slowly and deliberately. "Well, now you're gonna pay."

He broke into a run and barrelled into Thomas, knocking him to the ground and threw himself on top of him. Thomas grabbed Abraham's wrist, trying to hold it off as Abraham attempted to cut him. Abraham was winning, the bottle getting ever closer, less than an inch from his face. Pulling his wrist free, Abraham slashed the broken glass across Thomas's face and raised the bottle to bring it back down and do the same again.

A rage which had been building in Thomas for so long erupted like a volcano, a rage which increased when he caught the scent of eau de cologne mixed with breath that smelled strongly of whiskey. With a well timed jab of his knee in Abraham's groin and a forceful push, he succeeded in rolling his adversary over.

Thomas was now on top. Taken by surprise, Abraham released his grip on the bottle. Thomas grabbed it and slashed it forcefully across Abraham's exposed neck. In an instant, all the fight went out of Abraham. His eyes registered the shock that his jugular vein was open and life was fast leaking from him.

Trembling, Thomas stood up and dropped the bottle. It shattered. In a panic, he turned and ran, ran all the way home.

"What's happened?" asked Mosa, when he burst in, blood all over his face.

"I was attacked, in an alley."

"Sit down while I clean you up."

A patter of feet proceeded his sister who entered from the bedroom she shared with her mother. "Why are you bleeding?"

"He was set upon but he's gonna be all right. Get back to bed." Maisie, who was clutching a rag doll to her chest, didn't move. "Now! Or do I have to whip your ass?" Maisie scurried off.

"Did you see who it was?" whispered Mosa while she carefully dabbed her son's face with a cloth. The walls were flimsy and she didn't want Maisie to overhear their conversation.

"Abraham," replied Thomas in an equally quiet voice.

"Where's he now?"

"Lying in the alley, dead probably."

"Oh Lord." Mosa sank into the other chair.

"It wasn't my fault. He said I was gonna pay."

Mosa frowned. "Why didn't you just run like I always told you."

"I couldn't, there was a wall blocking off the end of the alley. He had me cornered."

"We've gotta get you out of New Orleans. A judge and jury won't believe you. You'll be found guilty, and you know what that would mean. Tomorrow I'll go down to the docks and get you a ticket."

"To where?"

"Up North."

"But I don't wanna go up North," protested Thomas.

"You don't have a choice." Mosa stood up, her eyes opaque and uncompromising. "I'll fix you something to eat, and then you need to go hide in the Backswamp. The police could be here any moment. You can come back tomorrow evening, after dark."

The enormity of the situation pressed down on Thomas and his shoulders sagged. "It ain't fair."

"No, it's not but we can't change that."

The next day, they came. They didn't bother knocking. They kicked open the door making Mosa jump.

"We've come for your son," said the first of the two policemen to enter.

"He's not here, he didn't come home last night. He must've stayed over at a friend's place." Mosa hoped the inner anxiety reflected in her voice wouldn't arouse suspicion. "Why you looking for him?"

"He killed somebody. Plenty of people saw him go outside during a break. He never came back in. A body was found in the alleyway outside. Turns out it was the man who gave evidence against him in his trial. You don't need to be a sleuth to work out what happened."

Mosa placed her hand over her mouth to feign shock. The other police officer walked around, opening the cupboard and going into the bedrooms, his boots clomping loudly on the wooden floor. He shook his head when he reappeared.

The officer who'd spoken gave her a stern, penetrating stare. "Make damn sure you let us know if he comes here. Harboring a murderer is a felony."

When Maisie returned from school, skipping in with a child's innocence, Mosa asked her to sit.

"I've something I need to tell you, but first you must swear to never tell a living soul or your brother might be killed, and I'll probably end up in jail."

Maisie nodded solemnly.

Thomas appeared late in the evening.

"I've got you a passage tomorrow night on a ship going to New York. Come back here when it gets dark and I'll walk down to the port with you."

"No, I don't want you mixed up in this. I'll go alone in case I'm caught."

Mosa watched him wolf down the meal she'd put on the table for him. Her fine, handsome son would be but a memory after tomorrow. When she would see him again she didn't know. She bit her lip and shut her eyes to hold back the emotion that wanted to burst out of her.

The following evening she pressed a wad of banknotes into his hand.

"This will help you get set up. Maisie and I will come visit when it's safe to do so."

Mosa wanted to say they'd move to New York to join him but she wanted Thomas to have time to find his own way before they did that.

Two lines of tears ran down Maisie's face. It had been a wrench when he worked on the steamboat but at least he'd spent winters back in New Orleans. Her elder brother was her idol, taking the place of the father she'd never known. Life without him would be empty. She hugged Thomas so tightly that he had to prise her hands from around his waist when it was time to leave.

Once he'd departed, Mosa couldn't hold back the dam of her feelings any longer and wept.

During the days which followed, she lived on her nerves and barely slept, fearful Thomas hadn't made it safely to the boat. Expecting news of his capture, each knock at the door caused the hairs on the back of her neck to stand on end and her legs to become weak.

A week passed and there was no news of his arrest. Mosa began to relax, it seemed likely that he had got away.

CHAPTER 4

Several weeks passed before a letter arrived. When it did, Mosa tore it open and danced around the room with joy. Thomas had made it to New York and found a job and a place to live. There was little detail, only a few lines, but it was all she needed to know. Her son was safe which was what mattered.
"When can we go see him?" asked Maisie when her mother shared the news.
"Not yet. If the authorities heard we'd gone off to New York that'd make them suspicious. Remember, don't breathe a word, ever. If the police get to find out where he is, he'd be hauled back and hung. You'd be responsible for his death."
Mosa knew it was a harsh thing to say to a child but it was effective. Maisie was never once tempted to reveal their secret.
Mosa memorized the address and burned the letter. The police might return at any time and ransack her home. When it came to the inhabitants of Tremé, they didn't bother with formalities such as search warrants.
Questioned by neighbors, Mosa was obliged to

maintain the pretence she had no idea where he'd gone. They'd seen the police come to the house, and some had been interrogated and asked if they knew where he was hiding. That Thomas was accused of killing someone was common knowledge. They sympathized with Mosa. Black people were wrongly accused all the time.

Fortunately, there was nobody to post a reward for information which could have tempted anyone who might have seen Thomas. Although he'd visited late in the evening, folks in Tremé spent a great deal of time sitting outside, even after dark.

It also helped that Mosa was well liked. She'd helped so many of their children with their education, and without ever asking for a cent in return.

Before she wrote back, Mosa walked to Samuel's law office. A pleasant smell of leather and cigar smoke greeted her. He welcomed her warmly but with a furrowed brow.

"It's good to see you but I hope you're not experiencing trouble again, that's normally the only reason I get visitors." Mosa explained. "I'm so sorry but you did right to send him away. There'd be no justice for him here. How can I help?"

"I'm here to ask a favor. I worry if I keep getting letters from New York, the police might get to hear about it. Would you mind if I had him write here? I could drop by occasionally and pick them up. I don't expect him to write often."

Samuel placed his hands on his desk. "I'd love

to help but I can't. I don't know if Thomas told you, but I'm taking a segregation case through the courts right now and intend going all the way to the Supreme Court. The authorities would love any opportunity to take me down. I was broken into only recently. I came in to find my papers scattered everywhere but nothing was taken. I'm sure it was them, looking for something to discredit me with. They might well do it again."

"I understand." Mosa stood to go. "Good luck with the case. It makes me proud to think I played a part in making it possible for you to be an attorney."

Samuel rose also. "You certainly did. The case could hardly be more important. Either segregation will be ruled unconstitutional or it will remain with us for generations to come."

"I'll hope for the former but, given the way things have gone since Emancipation, I fear it'll be the latter."

Mosa spoke with Angelique who agreed to be her recipient for mail. When Mosa wrote back she instructed Thomas not to write unless he needed help or it was really important. In time, she'd move herself and Maisie up there to be near him. She planned on waiting a few years until the death of Abraham was a distant event the police would no longer care about and wouldn't investigate her departure.

Mosa's worries weren't limited to her son. She approached Angelique one morning after class.

"I'm not going to be able to help out as much as I have been doing. The money I had is almost gone and I need to find a paying job."

"I wish we could get more money from the City so you could join me as a paid worker, but they're trying to cut what little they already give us."

Mosa enquired at several schools but the answer was always the same. Those for black children had no funds to hire an extra teacher, and the white schools weren't interested in employing her, parents would object. Mosa decided she had no choice but to widen her search.

On a hot August day, she stood before one of the largest mansions in the Garden District mopping the perspiration from her brow with a handkerchief. Adjusting her rather flat, navy wide-brimmed hat one last time, she climbed the stairs to the verandah and knocked on the double doors. Mosa practised a smile to banish the gloom enveloping her. She hadn't expected to be working in a house again after so many years.

When Mosa was ushered into the living room, the lady of the house eyed her imperiously. Mrs. Augustine Dampierre, seated regally on a gilded chair, was the matriarch of one of the city's oldest families. One which could trace its ancestry back to the founding of La Nouvelle-Orléans by the French in 1718.

A long pearl necklace in three rows hung over her purple silk dress with a high lace collar. On her left side, she wore a diamond-encrusted broach in the shape of the fleur-de-lis. Auburn hair was piled high on her head and drop pearl earrings hung from her ears grown large with age. Her French ancestral blood was confirmed by a prominent nose with a distinctive bump. Mosa felt utterly drab by comparison in her plain black dress buttoned up to the neck.

"Well, you look suitable enough but your reference says you're a school teacher." The woman's voice was thin but her green eyes were piercing.

"Yes ma'am. Unfortunately there's no jobs available for the likes of me. I cleaned house when younger, and you can rest assured I'm a hard worker."

"You'll need to be. Before the invasion by the North there were ten of your kind working in the house. Now I've only two servants. I'll give you a trial. Hours are eight to six every day except Sunday. Be here Monday morning. You may leave." The woman rang the bell on the coffee table next to her.

Mrs. Dampierre rarely acknowledged Mosa after that. She was expected to remain unseen and unheard just like when she'd been a house slave at Old Oaks Plantation.

Mosa wondered why her employer would want to live in such a big house, all alone save for a cook, and a maid to dress her and attend to every other task Augustine Dampierre was too lazy to do for herself. Bessie, the maid, told Mosa the house was once filled with life. Mrs Dampierre's husband and son had both died some years ago, and she was estranged from her daughter over her choice of husband. She lived in Washington and never visited.

By the time Mosa made it back to Tremé of an evening, her feet were sore and her back ached as if she'd spent a night lying on the floor. She wanted nothing more than to curl up in bed. The first time she arrived home to find Maisie cooking dinner, Mosa wanted to cry with gratitude.

Mosa had been working at the mansion for a few years when Angelique appeared one evening, a letter in hand.

"I'll leave you in peace to read it."

Mosa took it from her with trepidation. Thomas had followed her instructions and not written after the first time.

Mosa hands were shaking and her fingers fumbled opening the envelope. She feared he must be in trouble. When she pulled out the letter, another item fell face down on the floor. Picking it up, she smiled even though her eyes misted over. Her son looked so handsome in his suit and wing collar shirt next to his bride in white. It was such a bitter sweet moment. Mosa was so happy for him yet sad she hadn't got to see him marry and watch his bride walk down the aisle.

When Mosa married Joshua she'd done so in her ordinary work clothes, with only a bunch of flowers picked from the plantation garden to indicate it was her wedding day. With the house and a barn full of cotton awaiting sale lost in the fire, a wedding dress was something they couldn't afford. And now she'd missed her son's wedding.

"Let me see," Maisie had appeared at her side and was impatiently tugging at the photograph.

"Wait." But it was too late, the sound of ripping shocked them both into a moment of silence. "Look what you've done! You've ruined it, get to your room."

The tear had split Thomas's bride in half. Mosa laid the two pieces on the dining table and placed them side by side, but it was difficult now to make out the face of her son's wife. Mosa screamed out in frustration. God had granted her only the most fleeting glimpse of her daughter-in-law.

Mosa's immediate desire was to quit her job and rush to New York but she knew she couldn't. Thomas had a wife to take care of now, and soon there'd probably be children. Mosa was determined not to let herself and Maisie be an added burden. Perhaps within five years, she told herself, she would have saved enough to ensure they could be self sufficient, even if it took her and Maisie a while to find work when they arrived.

When Maisie appeared at her side and said sorry, she hugged her daughter close.

CHAPTER 5

Mosa's favorite room in the Dampierre mansion to clean was the library. Along two walls were shelves of books. While she dusted them, she took time out to read a few pages. It took her mind back to her younger days when she'd first experienced the joy of reading, her imagination taking flight to another place and time, away from the prison that was the plantation before the Civil War.

Amongst the works of Shakespeare, Dickens, and Twain, she noticed novels by the likes of Voltaire and Hugo in their original French versions. It seemed Mrs. Dampierre must have inherited an ability to speak the language.

The library also offered Mosa an opportunity to keep herself acquainted with what was going on in Louisiana and the wider world. Mrs. Dampierre took 'The Picayune' which she'd often leave lying on the walnut desk by the window that overlooked the garden. Today's headline caught Mosa's attention.

'Supreme Court upholds Louisiana law'

Curious, Mosa sat down to read more. Her shoulders slumped while she read. Samuel's attempt to overturn segregation had failed. The Justices had adopted the fiction of 'separate but equal', ruling there was no violation of the Constitution so long as the facilities for each race were equal. Yet everybody knew schools, housing, and every other aspect of life were far inferior for black people.

The opening of the door caused Mosa to jump up. She didn't have time to fold the newspaper and return to its usual place on the desk.

"Reading my paper?" Mrs. Dampierre's rhetorical question conveyed an icy chill.

"I apologise, ma'am. I was interested because the lawsuit on the front page was argued by someone I once taught."

"Well, at least those in Washington reached the right decision for once."

"Yes, ma'am."

"Really girl, you don't have to agree with everything I say." Mosa bristled inwardly at being called a girl at her age but she couldn't object, not if she wanted to remain employed. Older black women were often referred to as 'Auntie' which was no better, and men as 'boy' or 'Uncle. "Surely what happened proves my point. Having separate schools didn't prevent your student going on to become a lawyer and taking a case to the highest court in the land."

Mosa knew that debating the matter would be futile. She'd never change the woman's beliefs ingrained in her since childhood.

Mrs. Dampierre's voice softened. "I've been wanting to have a word with you. My eyesight's deteriorating and my doctor tells me I must stop reading. Books are one of the few pleasures left to me. I'd ask you to read to me but you're too good at your present job. Bessie tells me you have a teenage daughter. I imagine you've educated her well."

"Yes, she's an intelligent child."

"Good. Would she be free to visit and read to me in the afternoons?"

Mosa welcomed the opportunity. Maisie needed something useful to occupy her time once morning school ended. Aimlessly drifting around Tremé after school like she did now could so easily see her fall in with the wrong crowd. Maisie said she wanted to be a teacher like her mother, but it would be a while until she'd be old enough to go to college. Without some direction in her life, Mosa feared her daughter might take the wrong path.

That evening when Mosa raised the matter at dinner Maisie was unimpressed. "I don't wanna go read to some cranky white woman."

Mosa was in no mood to back down after a hard day's work. "Listen to me, young lady, I've been working myself into the ground these past few years to give you a good life, so I don't expect no moaning. You'll do as I say. It's only for an hour a day, and what's more you'll be paid for it."

Maisie walked to the Garden District with her chin stuck out and a scowl as pronounced as a darkening afternoon sky working up to the torrential downpours that pounded New Orleans most summer afternoons.

Shown into the library, Maisie stood sheepishly by the open door.

"I don't bite," snapped Mrs. Dampierre. "Come closer child so I can get a proper look at you." Maisie approached, her hands clasped submissively together in front of her as if expecting to be reprimanded. Mrs. Dampierre moved forward in her chair, leaning on the cane she used for support "Hmm." The woman's exhalation was noncommittal. "Your mother tells me you're a good reader."

"Yes, ma'am."

"Well, let's see how you do. Go find me 'Oliver Twist' by Charles Dickens from that shelf over there. It's a long time since I read the book and I should like to hear it again."

Maisie was awed, she'd never seen so many books. In the schoolhouse, there were less than twenty, many with pages missing because those had been cheaper to acquire. Running an index finger along the spines, she located the novel.

"Do you know the story?"

"No," replied Maisie.

"Then you're in for a treat."

Maisie soon forgot about her reluctance to be at the

house. Thoughts of wishing to be out wandering through the charmless and dusty streets of Tremé, which turned into a muddy morass whenever it rained, were cast aside while she was swept up in the unfolding story.

"I think I'll keep you," announced Mrs Dampierre at the end of that first session.

Maisie found herself looking forward to each visit so that she could read the next instalment. And when she'd finished that book there was another fascinating tale to be read and so many more to come. A novel was the perfect escape from the mundane predictability of her everyday existence. And Mrs. Dampierre turned out to be less fearsome than she'd first appeared. She even praised Maisie.

"I think you have a natural talent for reading out loud."

When the woman dozed off, which she frequently did, her head flopping toward her chest, Maisie would read on in silence. She always left a bookmark at the point they'd reached so she could react quickly when her employer awoke and ignored the fact she'd been sleeping. Instead she'd berate Maisie.

"Why on earth have you stopped reading, girl? I'm not paying you to just sit there."

Maisie gave her earnings to her mother. Mosa took them, saying she would set them aside and return them to Maisie once she began her training to be a teacher.

CHAPTER 6

Not many weeks after Maisie first began reading to Augustine Dampierre, Angelique arrived at Mosa's one evening, her face animated.

"I've got some great news. Samuel came by today. He wants to help fund the school. I spoke to him about how much more we could achieve with another teacher and he's agreed to pay for that, subject to one condition. That you are that teacher!"

Mosa shot up from her chair and clapped her hands together. "Oh, that's wonderful news. I'll be so glad not to be walking three miles each way to work. I'm wearing out my shoes every couple of months."

Mrs. Dampierre was phlegmatic when Mosa gave her the news. "I'm sorry to see you go but you'll be doing more good in your new position. Just don't take your daughter away. She's a credit to you."

Mosa beamed with pride. Life hadn't been easy these past few years but finally things were coming good.

More good news arrived a few days later in the

form of a letter from Thomas to tell her she was a grandmother to Joshua born earlier that month. Mosa rubbed both her eyes to contain her tears of joy but also her regret that her husband, Joshua, hadn't lived to see this moment.

He'd missed so much not seeing his children grow. All because he'd fought for freedom. The freedom for everyone to vote, regardless of color, a right that had lasted for only a few years. The man had had the courage to stand up for his beliefs, but if you did that as a black man it made you a target for the forces of hate who seized power after Reconstruction and had no intention of ever letting go of it.

That evening, Mosa unlocked the wooden box hidden under the bed and counted her savings. Maybe not much more than a couple of years and there'd be enough for her and Maisie to head for New York, a city Mosa had lived in nearly three decades ago. She knew it to be no paradise but it wouldn't be worse than New Orleans and they'd all be a family again, living close to each other, and that would be so wonderful.

Life assumed an easy going amble, like a gentle breeze coming up from the Gulf. Mosa enjoyed teaching, she always had, and Maisie floated through her days on the optimism of youth and daydreaming about the novels she read.

When she arrived at the Dampierre household to be told the old woman was sick, Maisie experienced sadness. An unexpected affection for the grand old dame had grown. She'd become almost like the grandmother Maisie didn't have.

Directed to Mrs. Dampierre's bedroom, she looked at the small and shrivelled figure, propped up in bed with pillows. Her voluminous hair turned out to be an elaborate wig. Like a stuffed animal, it sat on a mannequin head on her dressing table. Mrs. Dampierre's real hair was completely white, short, and flat under a lace bonnet tied beneath her chin. Maisie's nostrils picked up the stale smell of a bedroom not recently aired.

"Don't look so horrified, girl. I'm not dead yet, and I don't intend to be any time soon. Go down to the library and bring up 'Little Women' by Louisa May Alcott.

It was an engaging story but Maisie wished they could read at least one book that was about people like her. It was as if her race didn't exist in the literary world, appearing only briefly as anonymous slaves or servants. People of no consequence and whose hopes and feelings authors paid not the slightest attention to.

"You could change that," said Mosa when Maisie complained to her mother. "You can become a voice for black America if you want to."

"Me?"

"Why not."

"But I can't write."

"Nobody can until they try."

Maisie took to writing in secret in her room, the

one she'd inherited when Joshua left and she'd no longer had to share a bed with her mother. Maisie wrote a short story. One afternoon she took it with her.

Mrs Dampierre, now recovered from her illness, was seated in the library, waiting.

Maisie coughed, clearing her throat to summon up the courage. "I've written a short story and I've brought it with me. I was wondering if you might like to hear it and tell me what you think."

"What's it about?" asked Mrs. Dampierre without enthusiasm.

"A young woman living in Tremé who-"

"You should read it to your own kind. It's not something I'd like. Now let's pick up where we left off yesterday, we were just getting to the best bit."

Maisie speculated whether the woman was so insensitive with everyone or just 'Maisie's kind' as she'd doubtless put it.

Her confidence undermined, Maisie didn't tell her mother about her writing or she'd insist on reading it and most probably lavish her with praise regardless of merit.

"Sit back down for a moment," commanded Mrs. Dampierre at the end of a session a few weeks later when Maisie stood to leave. "I have a proposition. My grandson, Émile, runs the family business. He has done so ever since his father passed. He's shortly going to Europe and has asked me to accompany him. Bessie is unwilling to go, she says she's terrified of the ocean. Of course, it's an irrational fear, she's never even been on it, but I can't talk her round. You people are easily frightened by anything out of the ordinary. But you're young and I wager not so timid. I therefore thought I'd offer you the opportunity of coming along, as my maid. You'd need to come and stay in the house for a few days while Bessie showed you the ropes." Maisie was so surprised she failed to respond. "Well, girl?"

Excitement blossomed inside her, excitement of the anxious kind. A trip to Europe. A chance to see the world beyond New Orleans. It was a daunting prospect for someone who'd never left the confines of the city.

"I...I..." Mrs. Dampierre peered at Maisie with growing impatience. She decided to grab the opportunity, it would never come again. "Yes, I'd like that, very much."

"Good, that's settled then."

"I'd need to ask my mother."

Mrs. Dampierre rang her little bell. "Ah, Bessie, have Jasper ready the carriage."

The inhabitants of Tremé stopped whatever they were doing to watch the carriage painted in a pale yellow pulled by two magnificent black horses. The rutted roads of the faubourg normally only provided passage for wooden carts and mules.

Mosa rose from her rocking chair on the veranda when the carriage came to a halt in front of her.

"Is something the matter?" she asked when Maisie emerged.

"No, Mrs. Dampierre wants a word with you, inside her carriage."

Mosa climbed in.

"Sit. I didn't want to get out and be seen here for reasons I'm sure you can understand. I need to ask you something." Mrs Dampierre proceeded to explain.

"How long would she be gone?" asked Mosa.

"A few months."

"I don't think that's possible, there's Maisie's schooling -"

Augustine Dampierre threw out a hand in dismissiveness. "Come now, I'm sure she's way ahead of her peers. Indeed, I expect few of them are still in school, and think of what she'd learn. I'll allow her time off to visit museums and other places of culture. Surely you don't want to deny her such a wonderful opportunity?"

"Well, put like that."

"Exactly. You may get out now."

Mrs Dampierre tapped her stick against the inside front of the carriage and it moved off throwing up a cloud of dust from the dry dirt.

"Well?" asked Maisie.

She flung her arms around her mother with delight when she nodded.

CHAPTER 7

"Just how much money does she have?"

"A lot," answered Bessie while she showed Maisie Mrs. Dampierre's jewelry. There were necklaces of pearls and of gold, rings of sapphires and rubies and emeralds, a silver tiara and much more. "This broach is the thing she treasures most, her late husband gave it to her as a wedding gift." Bessie took it from its box lined with green velvet. In the shape of a fleur-de-lis, its numerous diamonds sparkled in the sunlight coming through the window.

"Wow!"

"Exactly," said Bessie.

Maisie had spent the last few days shadowing Bessie, watching her attend to the needs of her mistress. Tomorrow, Bessie would help her pack large trunks for the many outfits Mrs. Dampierre wished to take.

Maisie needed only a small suitcase for her spare black uniform and a dress of pale blue and a matching hat for Sunday best. Yet the disparity didn't concern her. She was thrilled at the prospect of going to Europe. Although she'd been born in England, she retained no recollection of it, having returned to America when only two years old.

"Oh do stop fiddling, girl," admonished Mrs. Dampierre while Maisie attempted to pin the broach on her dress. "Émile will be here for dinner any moment. Move! I can do it quicker myself."
"I'm sorry ma'am."
"You'll improve I dare say. Come down with me so I can introduce you."
Maisie held Mrs. Dampierre's arm as they descended the wide staircase while the woman held the bannister with her other hand for added stability.
No sooner had they reached the bottom when Émile arrived, kissing his grandmother on both cheeks. Maisie lowered her eyes. It was what white folks expected. They'd usually scold you if you didn't.
"This is my maid, for our trip. Maisie's her name."
"Pleased to meet you."
Maisie looked up. "Pleased to meet you too, sir."
He had a certain 'Frenchness' to him and a confident air which bordered on arrogance. His hazel eyes held her gaze and Maisie lowered her head once more.
"That'll be all," said Mrs Dampierre. "I'll send for you when I'm ready to retire. Come, Émile." She took his arm and they went into the dining room.
Later that evening in her box like room in the

attic Maisie lay awake, she was too excited to sleep. They would spend several weeks in Paris and then travel to London, Mrs. Dampierre had explained while Maisie helped get her ready for bed. Maisie's small world was about to become considerably bigger than she'd ever imagined it would.

The following morning, Maisie sat next to the driver on his horse and cart transporting the Dampierre's luggage while Mrs Dampierre and her grandson led the way in their carriage. Already above the buildings, Maisie could see three funnels pumping smoke into a cobalt sky. At the dock, a band played while passengers embarked. It reminded Maisie of when she had come down here with her mother to wave goodbye to her brother when he boarded a Mississippi steamboat. She still missed him so. It had been years since he'd had to flee.

When the ship pulled away, Maisie realized the bonds anchoring her to New Orleans were fast unravelling. The money she'd make from being a full time maid over the next few months would bring forward the day she and her mother could leave to join Thomas. Her return to New Orleans would be only temporary. Those streets and the sounds and smells of her youth were soon destined to become her past.

Maisie watched their departure from one of the portholes in Mrs. Dampierre's comfortable first class suite. She and her grandson were out on the deck but segregation didn't allow Maisie to join them.

To be at Augustine Dampierre's beck and call, Maisie had a tiny room adjacent to hers but Maisie wasn't expected to be seen out in the corridors, except when going down to the bowels of the vessel to eat with other servants. Should she come across a white person on the upper floors she'd already been instructed how to behave - come to a halt, lower her head, and stand sideways against the wall to let them pass.

Once the ship left the Mississippi and entered the Gulf of Mexico, it began to pitch. Maisie, who was standing behind Mrs. Dampierre seated at the dressing table, became queasy and struggled to ignore it.

"Pay attention, girl, you almost stabbed me with my broach."

"Sorry, ma'am. The boat moved unexpectedly."

"Get used to it, we've fifteen days of this."

Fifteen days. Maisie regretted her decision to come but it was too late now. After Mrs. Dampierre departed for dinner, Maisie went to lie down but that only made her feel worse. She decided fresh air might help. At this hour, the guests would all be dining. She furtively made her way to the deck which should be deserted. The strong breeze which greeted her proved to be a good tonic even if the vastness and deep, impenetrable blue of the ocean made her heart race with trepidation.

"Hello, I didn't expect to find you here." The man's

voice startled Maisie.

"I...I felt a little unwell and thought the air might help as indeed it has."

"Me too," said Émile. "It takes a day or two to find your sea legs."

"I must be getting back. Good night, sir."

In her rush to return, Maisie took a wrong turning. She turned down corridor after corridor. Each one looked exactly the same. Droplets of sweat tickled her torso and she began to panic. Augustine Dampierre would be furious if Maisie wasn't in her room when she returned from dinner.

Dashing around a corner, she found herself looking down on the ballroom. Beneath pendulous chandeliers, couples danced while a black band provided the music. For a moment Maisie forgot her worry, mesmerized by the scene below, men in their tuxedos and the women in the most gorgeous of gowns. The spectacle produced a smile even though Maisie knew she would never be part of something like that.

"We really must stop meeting like this." Émile had appeared at her side.

"I got lost."

"Let me show you the way back."

"Thank you, sir."

He marched purposefully, forcing Maisie to half run to keep up.

"Here you are. I think in Paris we'll need to provide you with an escort or we may never see you again when you go out." He gave her a broad,

mischievous grin. "Well, good night once more."
While Maisie awaited the return of his grandmother, she found herself thinking of Émile. He seemed nice for a white person, charming in fact. And he had such an engaging smile. No, this is ridiculous. Put all such thoughts out of your mind, she scolded herself.

CHAPTER 8

Required to spend most of her time trapped in her claustrophobic and windowless room, Maisie found the days long. Her mistress had insisted on bringing many books which helped pass the hours when Maisie wasn't needed to attend to her every wish.

Maisie became engrossed in an English translation of 'Les Misérables', particularly as a large part of it was set in Paris. It seemed the poor there fared no better than New Orleans. They were downtrodden wherever they might live, concluded Maisie.

Each night, Maisie dressed Mrs. Dampierre in a fine gown. The woman had brought enough of them not to have the wear the same one twice for the entire voyage. After she'd gone to dine one evening, Maisie opened the large closet and admired the other dresses hanging there. She pulled out her favorite, made from silk and teal in colour. The bodice was decorated with beads which sparkled in the light of the gas lamps.

Holding it against her, Maisie glided around the room, imagining herself to be at a ball dancing with a handsome man. The face which appeared in her mind's eye was Émile's.

A sudden ripping sound abruptly ended her fantasy. Horrified, Maisie lay the dress on the bed to examine it. A tear a few inches long ran upward from the bottom on the left side. Chains of panic tightened themselves around Maisie. How would she explain this? She couldn't. She'd be fired and sent back home the moment they reached France.

The night Mrs. Dampierre asked Maisie to dress her in that gown, Maisie's hands trembled while she fastened the buttons at the rear. When Mrs. Dampierre stood in front of the full length mirror to admire her choice, Maisie crossed her fingers behind her back.

She couldn't settle all evening, the woman was surely bound to notice.

"There's a tear in my dress," exclaimed Mrs. Dampierre immediately upon her return.

"I...I.." Maisie couldn't get her words out.

"I must have caught it on something." Relief flowed through Maisie's veins. "We'll have to see about having it repaired when we reach Paris. Undo it, I'm tired and I want to get into bed."

When they reached the coast of France, Maisie was once again limited to a restricted view from a porthole. Their place of arrival looked much smaller than New Orleans.

She was glad to be back on dry land and to no longer feel constant movement beneath her feet.

Within an hour they were on a train heading for the capital. It was Maisie's first ride in a locomotive. Initially she gripped the seat, never had she been in anything which moved so fast. Soon she was enjoying the journey and watching the world pass by. Fields and stone farm houses were dotted across the verdant landscape and cows munched grass, oblivious to the passing train. It was all so different to where she'd spent her life.

Paris was definitely bigger than New Orleans, mile upon mile of buildings lined the railway tracks. The station was the biggest building of them all. Trains beside long platforms sent smoke up to a high curved roof supported by iron girders. It seemed incredibly modern to a teenager from Tremé.

They took a horse and carriage to their lodgings. Maisie sat opposite Émile and his grandmother. Maisie was enchanted by the grand boulevards of cream colored buildings. They were of a cohesive design, complimenting each other to create a harmonious whole. Only a generation earlier, Emperor Napoleon III had commissioned Baron Haussmann to make the city lighter and more beautiful. He had succeeded, creating the icon that Paris is today.

Émile had rented them a house near the Arc de Triomphe from which several avenues radiated. Maisie's room was on the top floor. When she opened the shutters, she was delighted to find she had a view of the Eiffel Tower, thrusting skyward above the roofs of the city like something out of a Jules Verne novel.

Only recently completed and at over a thousand feet tall, it had easily surpassed the Washington monument in America's capital to become the world's tallest building.

That evening, Maisie was spellbound to see the tower transformed into the blue, white, and red of the French flag by beams of light projected toward the hundreds of small gas lamps on the structure. The homesickness she'd experienced on the voyage flew out of the window, replaced by the thrill of being here in Europe, a whole new world waiting to be discovered.

Mrs. Dampierre kept to a routine of taking a two hour nap after lunch and told Maisie she was free to explore during that time. Her favorite excursion was to stroll along the Champs-Élysées. Lined by trees, it was the widest boulevard of them all. She would wander down to La Place de la Concorde with its Egyptian obelisk between two large and ornate fountains, and beyond through the gardens leading to the Louvre. She would have liked to visit the museum but by the time she got that far she needed to turn around.

In Paris, she discovered a heady freedom. Men moved aside, many tipping their hats and smiling at her. There was no expectation that she should move out of the way like back home.

Café owners, addressing her as 'Mademoiselle',

called her to sit at one of their tables. There didn't appear to be any 'whites only' signs. Although, there were few people with her skin color. Here, Maisie was someone exotic and she liked that. For the first time in her life, she felt special.

On occasions, she would abandon her plans for a walk and sit at a pavement cafe while drinking coffee and observing passers-by to a background symphony of bicycle bells and horses' hooves. It was something she could never have done in the center of New Orleans. Not only would she have been unable to sit down, but had she dared watch white folks it wouldn't have been long until she'd have been chastised.

A few days after their arrival, Mrs. Dampierre caught a chill and announced she would take to her bed. Even though she wasn't particularly unwell, a full time nurse was sent for to sit with her.

"My misfortune is your good fortune. You may have the entire day to yourself."

Maisie went up to her room to put on her one nice dress. She wanted to look her best for a day in Paris. Coming downstairs, she encountered Émile in the hallway.

"I hear you have the day off. Would you like to accompany me to the Exposition Universelle?"

"The what?"

"It's a World's Fair, celebrating the centennial of the French Revolution."

Many European countries with monarchies had

boycotted the exhibition, not wishing to mark a celebration of the overthrow and guillotining of Louis XVI and his Austrian wife, Marie Antoinette.

"Won't you mind being seen with me?" asked Maisie.

"This is Paris not New Orleans, the normal rules don't apply."

He led her across the street toward the Eiffel Tower. Close too it was even more impressive, a powerful statement of modernity.

"Shall we go up?"

Elevators were still rare, the latest thing. The Eiffel Tower had a double decker one in each of its four pillars which ascended on inclined rails. Maisie began to wish she had refused the invitation when she took her seat and left her stomach behind while they climbed ever higher. Reaching the second level, the ground already seemed too distant.

"We're not at the top yet," announced Émile enthusiastically. A vertical elevator sped them ever upward. "It's like we're birds." Émile's face radiated his delight.

Maisie shut her eyes hoping it would soon be over. But it wasn't. Half way up a change was required.

When they reached the top, Maisie peered cautiously down from their glass enclosure and quickly stepped back. The crowds milling around so far below were minuscule like ants, and the glass roofed pavilions on les Champs de Mars looked as if they were no more than children's toy buildings. Maisie exhaled with relief when they descended.

Returning to the second level, Émile proclaimed they would eat in one of the restaurants. "There's a Russian one, a Flemish one, an American one, and a French one, which is where we shall eat."

A waiter pulled out the chair for her. It was surreal to be eating in a room full of white people. Their glances weren't hostile, merely curious. Looking down at the array of knives and forks on the tablecloth, her chest tightened. She had absolutely no idea which ones to use. Watch what Émile does, her inner voice recommended.

"Shall I order for us?"

Maisie was grateful the worry of making a fool of herself had been removed. The meal was more refined than any she'd eaten. Foie gras followed by boeuf bourguignon.

"What do you think of Paris?" he asked.

"It's incredible."

"My thoughts exactly. It's my favorite place. I deal in art, and I can tell you there is nowhere like it. I have business to attend to this afternoon but tonight there's a parade. Would you like to come with me to watch?"

Her mouth full of crème caramel, Maisie could only nod her agreement.

She took advantage of the afternoon to visit the Louvre. The artistic wonders cemented her desire to find a way to return to this city, somehow. It was a place of possibility, somewhere it seemed that she would be judged by what she did and not for her pigmentation.

As a soft pink dusk caressed the sky, Maisie walked with Émile to L'Esplanade des Invalides to watch 'la fête de nuit'. She was enchanted to see Senegalese cavalrymen ride past on majestic horses. In New Orleans, a black man was rarely seen riding anything but a tired old mule and most certainly not dressed as a cavalryman.

Afterward came Indian and Chinese foot soldiers. Then Annamites from French Indo-China in scary masks, veiled women dancers from Algeria, Javanese dancers in golden robes, and people from the Congo, gyrating even more energetically than those who danced in Congo Square in New Orleans.

A Tonkin dragon writhing, rising, and falling was the climax of the parade, preceded by men and women waving banners, parasols and lanterns, and some banging on gongs. Maisie was utterly enthralled.

"Even better than Mardi Gras, wouldn't you say?" commented Émile.

"Oh, yes," replied Maisie, unable to stop grinning.

CHAPTER 9

Maisie couldn't sleep. It had been such an incredible day, one like no other. She lay staring at the ceiling, images of today chasing each other around her mind. Eventually she gave up trying to sleep, relit her bedside candle, and went to sit at the small table to compose a letter to her mother.

An unexpected noise made her start and she leaped to her feet. The handle on the door was turning. The door opened and Maisie suppressed a scream. He stood there in flickering shadow.

"I wanted to come and say how much I enjoyed our day." Maisie froze, he was advancing toward her. "I don't want it to end."

She retreated until she was against the wall, her hands pressed against it. Warm breath brushed her face as he lowered his face but it wasn't soothing, it was urgent and forceful. Maisie wanted to say stop but she was too confused and frightened to speak. He clamped his lips onto hers. When his arms wrapped around her and pulled her close, she could feel their power.

The next few minutes passed in a haze. Afterward,

she struggled to recall the detail. The weight of him hadn't felt unpleasant. But what he did hurt. Now she was alone again, she pulled her nightdress back down to cover herself and lay completely still as if paralysed, unable to believe what had happened.

Maisie thought about running but she had nowhere to go, no one to help her. She couldn't mention it to his grandmother. There wasn't a soul she could tell. There was nothing she could do.

Émile came to her room several nights after that. He whispered gently in her ear. He told her she was beautiful, gorgeous, that he'd spent the entire day thinking about her. He brought her gifts of chocolate and perfume. What he did began to feel pleasant.

He talked of moving to Paris to live, to be free of convention. Maisie started to wonder if he might mean what he said, if they might both stay in Europe and be together.

Whenever he passed her in the corridor, he smiled at her, a smile which seemed genuine. What had been frightening had become exciting, what had seemed impossible began to seem possible. She found it hard to concentrate. He was constantly in her thoughts.

"Whatever's gotten into you," complained Augustine Dampierre while Maisie read to her. "You keep stumbling on your words, it's jarring. Focus, girl."

Later that summer, they took the train to the coast and a boat to England. White chalk cliffs rising out of a milky turquoise green sea promised lightness of spirit which matched Maisie's mood. She concluded she must be in love. A love that was forbidden in Louisiana but which could possibly thrive in Europe.

London was undeniably grand, yet it was a grandeur which was formal and tight lipped. Buckingham Palace was huge but not attractive, and the chimes of Big Ben solemn.

The roads were clogged with horses and loud with the noise of their hooves. Some pulled double decker trams, others carriages. Boys of ten years old or less darted in and out of the traffic with wooden buckets, scooping up the piles of manure which otherwise would soon have overwhelmed the city streets.

The Dampierres settled themselves in a house in Mayfair. Émile didn't visit Maisie's room and no longer met her eyes on the rare occasions their paths crossed.

In London, he disappeared all day returning late in the evening. Important meetings, his grandmother said.

Maisie tried to persuade herself he must be tired, and preoccupied with his business dealings. But eventually she had to admit it. Whatever it may have been, it was over.

Her innocence was gone, stolen by him without a

thought for her. Reality had come running at her and knocked her down and trampled all over her. That the burden of her secret couldn't be shared made it even more difficult to bear but Maisie had no choice other than to get back up.

As often as she could, Maisie wandered through the verdant lungs of the city. Hyde Park, Green Park, and St. James Park were all within a short walk. The whispers of nature amongst the large and leafy trees were a balm for her inner turmoil and heartache.

London didn't charm her in the way Paris had. In London, people stared at her. No restaurateurs sought to attract her attention. Men barged past her, making no attempt to step aside.

A trip to London Zoo in Regents Park changed her ambivalence to outright dislike for this imperial city.

"Hey, you." The man's shout was rasping. Only a few feet away, he stood with his wife or girlfriend and another couple. "The monkey house is over there. It's time you got back to it." The others laughed. Maisie quickly departed.

One afternoon, to fulfil her mother's wish, she took an underground train to Tower Hill. It was an unpleasant experience. Smoke from the steam locomotive filled the carriages and stung her eyes and left specks of soot on her dress.

Glad to reach the surface, Maisie asked for directions. She passed by Tower Bridge which was nearing the end of construction, its distinctive towers at each end almost complete.

Beneath the bridge the Thames flowed past, brown and uninviting under a sky hidden from view by dull clouds. Ships lined the river banks as far as the eye could see. Here was the hub of the largest empire the world had ever known, an empire which depended upon a vast fleet of merchant vessels to keep it bound together.

Maisie entered the East End, a London that bore no resemblance to the West End and its impressive buildings and extensive green spaces. Narrow alleyways of miserable dwellings in long rows and packed tightly together revealed a maze of poverty. It reminded her of Dickens's 'Oliver Twist'.

She climbed a precarious external wooden stairway which emitted creaks of protest. Washing hung on a line strung across the narrow balcony. A rat ran in front of her and scurried out of sight. Pushing a damp sheet out of her way, Maisie knocked.

The woman who answered looked as tired and worn as the drying clothes. Her uncombed hair was gray and her black dress had faded with age.

"What do you want?" Her voice was sharp.

"You don't recognise me, do you."

The woman eyed the young, dark-skinned woman before her in a pale blue dress and matching hat, better dressed than anyone who was normally seen in this part of London.

"Wait a minute." A smile lightened the dour face. "It can't be, surely. Maisie?"

"Yes."

"My, you've grown up. Well, come on in and sit down. I'll make us a cup of tea while you tell me why you're here."

Maisie explained. "Mama asked me to drop by to see how you're doing."

"I'm doing just fine. I found me someone. He has a job down at the docks but I expect your mother told you that already. It keeps a roof over our heads so I can't complain."

Maisie thought Lowenna had become an old woman, but from her youthful vantage point anyone over thirty looked ancient.

'How's your mother and Thomas?"

"They're good."

"I'm glad to hear it. I do enjoy reading her letters." The smile left Lowenna's face. "Do you ever hear anything of my son, Abraham?"

"No, I'm sorry, we don't," lied Maisie. She hoped Lowenna hadn't detected the nervousness in her reply. "I really must be going, Mrs. Dampierre will be waking up from her nap any time now."

"But the kettle's almost boiled."

"I'd love to stay longer but I can't. She gets awful mad if I'm not back in time."

Maisie was pleased to leave. It felt wrong not to tell Lowenna but Mosa had been quite insistent. It'll only bring her grief and she's had enough in her life without us bringing her more, she'd said. Maisie disagreed, she thought Lowenna deserved to know her son was dead, and why. But now she never would.

By the time she reached Mayfair, Maisie was lightheaded. It was a muggy late summer's day and she'd rushed so as not to be late. Worried she might faint, she grabbed a lamp post for support until the sensation passed.

Augustine Dampierre tutted with irritation when Maisie entered her room. "Ah, girl. I was wondering if you'd forgotten all about me. We'll have to forego our reading today. I've visitors arriving for afternoon tea. Help me get ready, they'll be here in ten minutes."

Placing a wig on the woman's head, Maisie experienced a sudden rush of nausea. She ran from the room and only just reached the servants' bathroom in time.

"What's going on?" demanded an unimpressed Mrs. Dampierre on her return.

"I'm so sorry, it must be something I ate.'

"Well, I hope whatever you've got isn't contagious."

When Maisie was sick the following morning, a cold sweat broke out all over her body. No, this couldn't be happening... could it? She'd thought her clothes feeling tighter must be down to all the food she'd been eating in Europe, way more than she'd eat at home. What would her mother say, and even worse Mrs. Dampierre if she found out?

They were leaving on a boat for home in a couple of days, ahead of Émile who still had business to finish. If only she could hide her condition until they reached New Orleans.

CHAPTER 10

Aboard ship a few days later, Maisie vomited in the presence of Augustine Dampierre while helping her get ready for dinner.

"What on earth? The ocean's as calm as can be. Wait a moment… you're not, are you?" Eyes ablaze with accusation and indignation, Mrs. Dampierre glared at Maisie who hung her head. "I thought I'd trained you to be respectable. How foolish I've been. My daddy used to say, never get attached to a nigger, they'll always disappoint you. Just when you think you've civilized them, they revert to type. They're savages, they always were and always will be. How right he was." Maisie kept her head down.

"When did this happen, in Paris?"

Maisie managed a nod.

"And who's the father?"

The name stuck like a pebble in Maisie's throat.

"Answer me, girl!"

"Émile." The quiet release of the word exploded in the room as if a bomb had gone off.

"You filthy whore! Seducing my grandson. You

disgust me. Clean up your mess and then get out of my sight."

The rest of the voyage passed in a glacial silence. A silence broken only by the orders Mrs. Dampierre gave whenever Maisie was summoned from her side room by bell. Not once did the woman deign to make eye contact with Maisie.

Mosa noticed instantly Maisie entered the house..
"I'm sorry, Mama."
Mosa hugged her daughter while she sobbed. "Sit down and tell me how this happened."
"But why didn't you just say no," said Mosa after Maisie explained.
"I don't know why. I was scared. And then when he kept visiting me I kidded myself that he really had feelings for me, that we'd live a life together in Paris. I know it sounds crazy."
Remembering the sense of powerlessness when she'd been raped by her half brother, Jefferson, Mosa didn't berate her daughter. Maisie had been alone and defenseless and so far from home.
"We can't change the past. We'll just have to make the best of it, but I'm not giving up my teaching job, we need the money. You'll have to learn to be a mother and forget about going to college until the child is older."
Maisie missed a breath. The repercussions of her situation tightened around her. Her world, which only a few months ago had offered such promise and excitement, was shrinking to be smaller than

it had ever been.

She didn't want this baby. She didn't want to be tied down by motherhood. And she wanted freedom, true freedom, not the myth of freedom on offer in New Orleans.

In her windowless, and coffin-like room on the voyage home, Maisie had spent a considerable amount of time thinking. She had devised a plan. She gave her mother a few days to get used to the idea of the pregnancy before broaching the subject.

"Paris could offer us a better life."

"Whatever do you mean?" Mosa frowned while she pummeled dough with floury fists to make bread.

"The French are just as bad, they had slavery too. Talk to the Haitians here and they'll tell you how brutal the French were. How they impoverished that country and its population of former slaves by forcing the Haitians to pay millions in reparations to avoid bombardment for having risen up against the French and driving them out."

"Well, all I know is Paris ain't like here. I was treated as if I was white. They don't have separate stores or restaurants for the different races. Over there even the cavalry are black. We could have a better life in France, one where we could do whatever we wanted and not live in constant fear. We could take French lessons when we got there, we'd soon get the hang of the language."

Mosa wiped her hands on her apron, and stared at her daughter as if she'd lost her mind."Absolutely

not. When we've saved enough, we're moving to New York to be near your brother and that's that."
"But-"
"No buts, this conversation is over, and I don't want the subject ever mentioned again. Now make yourself useful and wash the dishes."

The birth exhausted Maisie and she fell asleep as soon as Mosa handed her the child. When Maisie woke, she examined her baby girl lying on her chest and inhaled sharply. Her appearance was a shock, skin so pale she could pass for white.
"How can she be this color?"
"Her daddy's white but I agree you'd expect her to be darker," answered Mosa. She pursed her lips before continuing. "There's something I never told you. Both my parents, your grandparents, were white." Maisie's mouth dropped open in astonishment. "My color is a throwback to generations earlier, from an African male."
"Then why were you a slave?"
"Because they didn't want to acknowledge me as their own, it would've ruined their reputation. You know how it is. But whatever color your daughter is, she's beautiful and precious, and yours to look after and protect. Have you thought what will you call her?"
Maisie didn't hesitate. "Josephine."
"A French name?"
"Yes, it'll remind me of the few weeks I had when life seemed full of promise."

Mosa sighed. "Life is what you make it. You make your own happiness. Just be grateful you have a healthy baby."
But Maisie didn't experience joy or love for her child. The only emotion she experienced was resentment. And as if life wasn't going to be difficult enough, Josephine's color would present more problems.

Not many weeks after Josephine arrived, the yellow carriage drew up outside the house once more. Mrs. Dampierre entered without knocking. Maisie stood, cradling Josephine in her arms. The woman winced at the sight of her great granddaughter.
"I'll be brief. I haven't come to see the child. Here, take this." She thrust an envelope at Maisie. "There's five hundred dollars in there. I want you and your baby to leave New Orleans and never come back."
"But-"
"I've given you more than enough to make a start somewhere else. Stay and there'll be serious consequences."
Climbing back into her carriage Augustine Dampierre stumbled and caught herself against the door. She failed to notice what she'd left glinting in the dust.

CHAPTER 11

While they prepared the evening meal, Maisie told her mother the news. "The old witch came today and gave me five hundred dollars. She said to leave town or there'd be consequences."

"Well, I don't like us being threatened but with what I've saved it'll be enough to join your brother. I'll speak with Angelique in the morning to see how long they need me to stay until they can find a -"

Mosa didn't get to complete her sentence, distracted by a sudden rush of air as their door was flung open. She was confused to see two policemen in their double breasted blue uniforms. Her immediate thought was they must have found out that Thomas was in New York.

"Maisie Elwood," pronounced one, "we have reason to believe you have taken Mrs. Dampierre's diamond broach."

"I don't know what you're talking about," she replied.

"She was wearing it when she arrived here this morning. On the journey home, she discovered it was gone. You need to give it back."

"But I don't have it. Maybe it fell off in the street or when she got home."

"It's not lying on the ground outside, we already looked, and she doesn't have it so this is the only place it can be. We'll need to search the house."

They didn't wait for permission. Thorough, they showed no regard for Mosa's property, emptying drawers on the floor and pushing the beds on their sides. Frightened by the clatter, Josephine began screaming. Mosa picked her up from her wooden crib to comfort her.

"What have you done with it, did you sell it already?" accused one of the men.

"No, of course not. I never had it. She was wearing it when she left," protested Maisie.

"You better come up with a better story than that for the judge. You're under arrest."

"What? Just because the broach is lost doesn't mean she took it," protested Mosa.

"Shut up, or we'll arrest you, too, for obstructing officers of the law."

Mosa could only watch in dismay while they grabbed her daughter's arms and placed handcuffs on her and then pushed her outside and into the waiting carriage.

Samuel arrived at his office the next morning to find Mosa outside the building, a baby in her arms. "She's Maisie's, my daughter's," she said in response to his quizzical look. "Her white boss took advantage of her. I need your help."

"Of course, let's go inside."

After listening, he leaned back in his green leather chair and placed his hands together in front of his mouth as if praying.

"Is it bad?" asked Mosa anxiously. "Maisie doesn't have it. The woman clearly lost it elsewhere"

"You've seen how our justice system works. Proof is optional when it comes to us folks. I'm happy to represent her pro bono, but the white jurors will almost certainly find her guilty with or without the broach or money to show she sold it. If they're in any doubt, the fact she's an unmarried mother will seal her fate. I wouldn't even put it past the prosecution to claim the money Mrs. Dampierre gave Maisie was what your daughter got for selling the broach. You need to prepare yourself and Maisie. She's likely to get ten years."

Mosa groaned.

"I hate being the bearer of bad news but I wanted to give it to you straight. There's also a strong likelihood they'll take your granddaughter away when they put her mother in jail. She'd be given to a white family to use as a servant when she's older. They wouldn't pay her much if at all, claiming they needed to recover the cost of keeping her when she was too young to work."

Mosa looked down at the helpless infant in her arms. Josephine stared at her grandmother with an expression of complete trust. Mosa knew what she must do.

Before entering, Mosa turned and looked down the street. People were going about their business, and then home to their loved ones. It would be a long time until she got to do that again.

"Yeah?" The officer at the desk eyed her with irritation for interrupting his day.

"Sir, you've arrested my daughter for stealing jewelry, a diamond broach belonging to Mrs. Dampierre. But it wasn't her, it was me. I saw it lying in the street outside our house when I got back from teaching at school. I picked it up and went off and sold it to pay off some debts I ran up."

The man didn't question her account. "Hey, go release that young nigger woman they brought in last night. It was her mom who did it, she's come to confess." He shouted down the corridor.

When Maisie appeared, her brow wrinkled in confusion. "What's going on Mama?

"It's okay, it's for the best. Here, take Josephine and get on home. Mama loves you, loves you both."

She pushed the infant into her mother's arms.

"Wait," called Maisie. But the officer was already leading Mosa away. She didn't turn around. She didn't want Maisie to see the trail of tears running down her cheeks.

Several other women already occupied the small cell. Their clothes were a lot fancier than Mosa's and their makeup gaudy. They eyed her curiously, in her prim and proper drab, gray dress.

"What you gone done?" asked one. "I can't imagine

you work the streets looking like that unless you give it away." The others laughed.
"I stole a diamond broach from a white woman."
"Too bad you got caught, honey. I bet you deserved to have it more than she ever did."
Mosa lowered her head hoping to end the conversation and take the attention away from her. It had the desired effect, they ignored her and continued their own conversation.

Samuel visited. They were only allowed to talk through the bars of the cell.
"Maisie came to see me and asked me to help you. I've spoken to the officer in charge here and have details of your confession. You're a brave woman."
"I'm a mother and grandmother. I need to do whatever it takes to protect my family."
"I can make a plea in mitigation on your behalf, it might reduce the sentence."
"I doubt it. There's one thing you can do for me, though."
"Name it."
"Go visit Maisie and tell her to take the money Augustine Dampierre gave her and go to New York and join her brother. Could you also help organize her trip?"
"Of course, I'd be glad to. And when you get out if you need anything, and I mean anything, you know where to find me."
Her cell mates whistled when Solomon left.
"My, you sure are a dark horse. Where'd you find a

tall, handsome man like that?"

"It's a long story."

"I bet it is but we got plenty of time. In fact, time is all we got."

Mosa appeared in court the next day. The same court where she'd watched Thomas tried and nearly convicted and sentenced to death for a crime he hadn't committed.

Pleading guilty, it was all over in minutes. There was no need for a trial. The judge brought his gavel down with what seemed like relish. He sentenced Mosa to ten years, exactly as Samuel had predicted. Later the same day while those on the sidewalks stopped to watch the line of shackled prisoners, Mosa was led down to the Mississippi where she was pushed into the hold of a boat going up river. Her fellow passengers were nearly all black and male and already dressed in a prison uniform of black and white horizontal stripes which fitted loosely like pajamas. Prison uniforms for women hadn't yet been introduced and Mosa still wore her own dress.

The experience reminded her of when she'd been transported to Macon, Georgia, as a slave. And once more she'd be a slave. The Thirteenth Amendment, ending slavery, allowed that heinous condition to continue to exist as punishment for a crime. Mosa's life had gone full circle.

The journey took days. The heat and humidity in the bowels of the vessel were overpowering. Most of the time the hatches above, which might have allowed some breeze to penetrate the prisoners' airless dungeon, were kept closed. Mosa's head throbbed continuously and the hot, putrid air she had to breathe made her want to retch.

She couldn't recall having ever felt so unclean. Her indignity was total. Mosa was obliged to use the same overflowing buckets as the men and in full view of them. To save her daughter, she'd entered the gates of hell.

Mosa fought sleep. When her eyelids closed or her head dropped forward onto her chest, she forced herself to wake up. At times, she failed and woke with a jolt, her heart racing in panic.

She might be fifty and no longer young and attractive but she was still afraid. In the darkness only the whites of eyes were visible, eyes which stared at her intently like wolves, watching and waiting.

If any man made a move, she knew screaming would be pointless. The guards wouldn't care. The law offered black folks precious little protection on the outside, and once a convict there was none.

Despite the heavy weight of misery which crushed her spirit and made her want to weep, Mosa was glad her daughter wasn't here. Prisoners in chains might struggle, but when a woman was in jail there'd be plenty of opportunity for the prison guards and no one to stop them.

CHAPTER 12

Angola. The word struck fear into Louisiana's black population. Notorious then as it is today, bearing the shameful distinction of being America's worst penitentiary. Survival rates were appalling, a seven year sentence was considered equivalent to a death sentence because that was the average length of time before a prisoner in Angola died.

In the era of slavery, owners paid attention to keeping their slaves alive. They were needed to work the plantations and cost money to replace. The new system of convict labor didn't need to concern itself about preserving life. Louisiana's penal system, designed to provide free black labor, could be relied upon to provide an endless supply of workers using mass incarceration as its recruiter.

A former Confederate officer, Samuel James, had purchased Angola. He quickly turned it into a money making machine, leasing out prisoners to surrounding plantations which he then also bought with his profits. Four fifths of the prisoners were black, and they suffered much worse treatment and conditions than the white inmates. It was in this dystopia that Mosa was condemned to serve her sentence. The women were put to work cooking and cleaning while the men labored in the fields. Through the kitchen window, she watched the long, sorry column walk out at dawn accompanied by prison guards on their horses. And she watched them return at dusk, feet shuffling, heads bowed, their utter exhaustion palpable.

"Makes you think, don't it?" commented Bertha, one of her fellow prisoners, who was standing beside her. "It's as if the last thirty years never happened, as if the War never happened. The Confederates knew those in Washington would eventually get tired of trying to change things and let them revert to the old ways. Anyway, we ain't got time to stand around, they'll be hungry. Come on."

Mosa doled out meat and gravy to the men in line as they passed her, mainly gravy because the meat supplied wasn't enough to feed even half the number it was supposed to. Still, it was better than most days when there was no meat at all.

At night, the women slept in their own dormitory. But nighttime provided no escape to a land of dreams. The turning of the key in the lock had them all on edge. Sometimes it was only a guard checking up on them, sometimes not. An arm grabbed, a bed left empty, and on return the sound of crying or the shock of silence.

Silence was the reaction of Salome, the young woman in the bed next to Mosa. She wasn't much older than Maisie. Sent here for the crime of being poor, stealing because she was hungry. Mosa reached out in the darkness and held her hand in an attempt to comfort her, though Mosa knew the trauma would haunt Salome forever.

Mosa tried not to think how long she was going to be incarcerated. If she thought of the years it was overwhelming, a void separating her from her family which she might never cross. By the time of her release, her granddaughter would be ten and Mosa sixty. If she ever made it to New York, it would be more than fifteen years since she'd seen her son. Mosa wished she had something to stop her contemplating life running away from her while her time left on earth steadily decreased.

"What was it you did before you ended up here?" asked Bertha while they were both down on their hands and knees scrubbing the wooden floors.

"I taught in a school in Tremé."

"A teacher. Maybe if I'd had me an education I wouldn't have ended up here."

Bertha planted a seed that grew, grew until Mosa could ignore it no longer and summoned the courage to request a meeting with the prison governor.

"What do you want?" His voice was gruff and his eyes angry when Mosa entered his office.

"Sir, most here can't read or write. I was a teacher in New Orleans. I was thinking that in the evenings I could teach-"
"Thinking," he interrupted her. "Niggers thinking instead of doing what they're told is dangerous. No one here needs to know how to read or write so forget your stupid notion about educating them and get out of here."
The man had the blinkered attitude of an overseer on a slave plantation, a compete disdain for the prisoners. They were getting what they deserved and their treatment should reflect that.

In Tremé, Maisie missed her mother. She bitterly regretted all that had happened. If she'd never gone to Paris her mother wouldn't be in jail, and the little creature who never stopped bawling for more than a few minutes when she put her down wouldn't exist. Maisie wouldn't be constantly tired and drained of energy. Instead, she could be pursuing the life she wanted, not this dismal existence of unending drudgery.

She left Josephine inside to cry and sat with her legs dangling over the verandah, examining the ticket. The small suitcase was packed. Soon they'd be leaving for the station and the long journey to New York.

When she turned the ticket over to look at the rear of it, it slipped from her hands. A gust of wind blew it under the verandah. Maisie jumped down to retrieve it.

The ticket was lurking under the house beyond the steps, taunting her. Maisie stretched her arm out toward it but the piece of paper was still a long way from her grasp. She slid her head under and then her upper body. It was a tight and uncomfortable squeeze. Dust blew in her face and she tasted grit in her mouth. With the tips of her fingers Maisie managed to touch the edge of the ticket and then slide it toward her.

Turning her head while she slithered backward to extricate herself, Maisie halted. Under the steps behind a wooden support, there it was, the cause of their recent trouble. If only she'd slid under the house when she'd looked around weeks ago.

Maisie didn't care that her best dress was now smeared with dirt. She'd found it and that was all that mattered. Her mother would be released and they'd leave for New York, together.

Leaving Josephine unattended, Maisie half ran and half marched across town, exhilarated by her discovery. To think she could have left not even knowing it was there, beneath their feet all this time. She clutched the object of so much misery in her hand, determined it shouldn't go missing again.

Divine intervention must surely have caused the ticket to fall from her hand. "Thank you, Lord," she whispered looking up at a bright blue sky of hope. She'd have her mother back and life would be easier. Perhaps when they got to New York, her mother would relent and let Maisie pursue her dreams while she looked after the baby, or maybe Maisie could get Thomas's wife to take care of her. A life without options no longer obscured the horizon.

"Honey chile, what are you doing here?" asked an astonished Bessie when she opened the door. "She don't ever wanna see you again."

"Tell her I found the broach," said Maisie breathlessly, "but she ain't getting it unless I can give it to her in person."

When Bessie returned, she nodded and escorted Maisie to the living room. Augustine Dampierre was seated in her chair, like a queen on a throne. She wrinkled her nose as though Maisie were the source of an unpleasant smell.

"I found the broach, ma'am." Mrs. Dampierre swiftly snatched it from her outstretched hand and surveyed it for damage of which there was none. "It was under the steps going up to the verandah. I don't know how nobody saw it before. It must've rolled there when it came off your dress. Anyway, you can tell the police you've got it back and they can set Mama free." Augustine Dampierre didn't respond. "Ma'am?"

"I heard you," she snapped.

"I'd be mighty grateful-"

"If you're telling the truth, your mother lied to the police. That's a serious felony. You've probably had the broach all along. I expect you and your mother intended selling it when it was safe to do so. When things didn't work out as you planned, you came here pretending you found it lying in the dirt."

"But that's not true," protested Maisie.

"Don't take that tone with me, girl. And what are you still doing here? I told you to leave New Orleans."

"I am, I have a train ticket for New York. I was due to leave today."

"Well, make sure you do or I'll be reporting you to the police, and you'll be joining your mother."

She rang her bell. "Bessie, escort her out."

While she walked home, Maisie wiped tears of frustration from her cheeks with the back of her hands. The promise of a better tomorrow denied by that mean spirited woman. Maisie couldn't understand how she could be like this. She wanted for nothing so why did she want to ruin the lives of those who were so much less fortunate?

Later that day with Josephine tied to her back and suitcase in hand, Maisie turned and took one last wistful look at the house. Once it had been filled with love and echoed to laughter but no longer. It was an empty shell containing only the ghosts of memories of happier times.

CHAPTER 13

Mosa couldn't help but think of Maisie whenever she looked at Salome. Salome had the same ebony skin, though her face was fuller and rounder and her nose wider. Every minute of every day Mosa missed her daughter, but witnessing what she had the other night once again made her thankful Maisie wasn't incarcerated here.

Mosa took Salome under her wing. They worked together and ate together. Salome didn't talk much but over time she told Mosa of how she'd ended up at Angola.

Salome came from Baton Rouge. Her father, one of the few black people there who owned land, farmed a small plot that was big enough to feed Salome and her two younger sisters. Their mother had died giving birth to the youngest one.

The local landowners didn't like having a black man owning property outside their sharecropping system. He'd been offered money to sell his farm, much less than it was worth, and he'd refused. So they tried intimidation instead. When they came at night and set fire to his crops, he tussled with them. Salome witnessed him being shot.

"Tell anyone who did this and we'll kill you and your sisters," the ringleader threatened her.

Flames still lit up the night with an orange glow when Salome began digging her father's grave. By the time she'd made a hole large enough a blood colored ball of sun was breaching the horizon.

Her muscles protesting and her vision clouded by tears, she rolled his body to the edge and pushed it in. Shoveling earth upon her father seemed so disrespectful but Salome had no choice, she was too poor to afford a coffin. While she covered the man in dirt she fought back thoughts of worms and maggots eating away at him, but for weeks nightmares of that and of his murder would plague her.

With nothing to feed her sisters and no money to buy food, Salome had reached through an open window and taken some cornbread. Its deliciously fresh cooked aroma was irresistible to a girl who hadn't eaten in days. A man across the street saw her and dragged her by the hair to the police station.

"What'll you do when you get out of here?" asked Mosa.

"Go find my sisters and try to go North. I heard life is better there."

"It can be. I worked in New York once. Though there's plenty of white folks up there who don't like us but, yes, I'd say it's not as bad as the South. Did you get an education?"

"No, daddy needed me to take care of the house."
"I was a teacher. How'd you like to learn to read and write? It'd give you a step up when you do get out."
"You'd do that for me?"
Mosa nodded, the prison governor wouldn't achieve total victory after all.
There were no books or paper at Angola so Mosa improvised. Whenever they got the chance, the two of them would slip behind the dormitory. Using a stick she kept hidden underneath the building, Mosa scratched letters in the dirt. When they heard footsteps they'd quickly rub the letters out with their feet.
Night was the worst time. The time when guards with bad intentions came. Salome would fall silent and tremble. Mosa's heart ached that there was nothing she could do to protect her. The only law in Angola was the law of the jungle. If a predator was on the prowl there was nowhere to hide. Fortunately, Salome was left alone and they both relaxed, a little.

"We're gonna need y'all out in the fields this week," barked one of the guards when he stormed into the women's dormitory at sunrise. "The cotton needs picking and we're short of men. The boss hired out too many to the other plantations."
Mosa welcomed the prospect of a change, being outside instead of cooped up all day cooking and cleaning. But the reality was worse, they still had to cook meals when they returned late afternoon,

hot, sweaty, and weary from their toils.

While she picked, Mosa observed the scene around her. It was as if time had stood still. It looked no different to when she was young. Black folks, sacks hung from their shoulders and bent over bushes, working from sunup to sundown and earning not a single cent for their labor.

"Hey, you! Keep picking." A guard, rifle slung over his shoulder, approached. When he reached her, his eyes lingered but not on Mosa. Salome looked down at the ground but she could sense his intense gaze.

"Was that the one?" asked Mosa after he moved on.
"No, I don't think so."

The next day he returned, his eyes rapacious.
"I need you to come with me." Salome didn't move.
"That's an order, not a request."

Mosa watched her walk beside his horse toward the trees. The man jumped down, tethered his horse to a tree and pulled Salome roughly by her arm and out of sight.

Mosa looked about her. No other guards were nearby. She headed for the trees.

They hadn't gone far into the forest. He had Salome pinned to the ground, inflicting his horror. The man encapsulated the hatred and abuse Mosa had endured her entire life. She couldn't stand by any longer and look away and pretend like nothing was happening.

Grunting like a pig, he didn't hear her. Picking up

the rifle he'd laid down on the earth beside him, she held it by the barrel and swung it with all the force she could muster into the back of his head, again and again. The sound of a shattering skull stilled his feral noises.

Mosa shoved him off Salome and onto his back. His eyes remained open and surprised but there was no life left in them.

"What do we do now?" asked Salome. Mosa stood immobile as if under a spell. "Mosa? They'll hang us for this if they don't shoot us first."

Hang. Shoot. The words brought Mosa back from wherever her mind had taken her.

"This way." They went deeper into the forest, Mosa leading. How long a start they'd get she didn't know but even a good one might not be enough. They had dogs, vicious dogs, dogs that could run faster than either of them could.

Mosa remembered the dogs when she tried to escape from Old Oaks Plantation, the barking and snarling, and how they'd caught up with her. Once more she was having to run because of the white man's violence. The skin on her back was still hideously marked from the whipping she received back then.

"Why'd you have to kill him?"

"I only meant to knock him out." Mosa knew that wasn't true, she'd wanted him to die. It was one crumb of justice in a world buried deep in injustice. "Anyway, what's it matter, either way we'd have met the same end."

"You maybe."

"Oh, so you just wanted to let him do that to you," snapped Mosa.

"It's better than being hung."

Salome's lack of gratitude annoyed Mosa. She sought to channel her anger into moving forward and staying alive. Arguing would ensure they were captured and dragged back, tied to a horse, struggling to keep up, falling in the dirt and being pulled along like carcasses.

Soon their clothes were wet with perspiration and their tongues dry as sand in their mouths. Both listened while they ran, listened for that first bark of impending doom.

Ahead through the gaps in the trees they saw the forest ending. But their route offered no escape. Flowing wide and deep, the Mississippi blocked their way.

CHAPTER 14

Mosa dropped to her knees by the river bank. She leaned forward and scooped water up with her hands. The cool liquid ran down her parched throat bringing a brief moment of bliss.

"Where now?" asked Salome.

"Along the river bank. If we hear them, I'm jumping in. I'd rather drown than be beat up and lynched."

Salome gave her a solemn look that belied her youth. "Me too. I'm sorry about what I said earlier. Thank you for what you did. A life at Angola is no life. At least if we die, there'll be no more fear, no more pain or sorrow. Jesus will take us to a land of milk and honey where color won't matter."

"Amen," agreed Mosa. "But before we give up on this earth, let's get moving." She still hoped for a miracle, Mosa didn't want her life to end this way. It was too soon, she wanted so much to see her family again.

Rounding a bend in the river, they halted but it was already too late. The man sitting on the river bank stared at them.

"Good day to you."

Mosa quickly assessed the situation. The man with a wide-brimmed straw hat and skin of leather baked from life under a hot sun was probably older than she was but bigger and stronger. However, his skin color was a relief.

"The name's Solomon."

"I'm Mosa and this is Salome. Is that your raft?"

Tied to a tree by the water's edge a log raft, on the rear of which was a small tent, offered salvation.

"Yes ma'am, I live on the river. It's the only place I ever found freedom. Nobody's able to boss me out there on Ol' Man river."

Mosa saw no point beating about the bush, he'd either say yes or no, and if no they needed to keep running. "Any chance we could hitch a ride?"

"Where to?"

"Wherever you're going."

"Is you two on the run?"

"Yeah, we escaped Angola, put in there for crimes we didn't commit."

"Tell me about it. I too spent time locked up. I'm going south with the current. Hop on board. But I'll need you to get in the tent, at least until we gone a few miles. I don't wanna be arrested for harboring fugitives."

The tent was cramped. There was nowhere to sit other than on a worn mattress with their knees bent up against their chins. The remainder of the space was filled by wooden crates which contained clothes, canned food, a cooking pot, a metal bowl, and other utensils.

The air was stuffy and didn't smell good either but they didn't care. Second by second they were steadily floating away from their pursuers, and the hounds would be unable to pick up their scent out here on the water.

Come dusk, Solomon opened the flap of the tent. "I usually tie up somewhere quiet at night so I can get me some rest, but I reckon tonight we should keep on going, though you can come out now."

The sun had already set and darkness was creeping in from the east obliterating the brushstrokes of crimson and mauve painted across the sky. Mosa inhaled the fresh air and let the soothing ripple of the water revive her. Darkness might be coming but in her world day was breaking. The long night which Angola had ushered in was ending. Mosa dared to hope she was going to make it north to New York and be reunited with Thomas and Maisie.

Solomon pulled in the line he trailed behind the raft. A catfish slithered around on the deck. "We'll stop at dawn and cook him. If you're hungry there's cans of peaches in the tent."

There was silence while they ate. The fruit tasted heavenly and something that had never been on the prison menu.

"How far south are you going?" asked Mosa.

"I'll turn around just before New Orleans. I don't care much for big cities. There's always trouble lurking in them places."

Mosa suppressed a cry of joy. Today was turning into something akin to a miracle. She'd keep to the outskirts of the city and make her way to Tremé, retrieve the savings she'd hidden, and take a boat out.

"How far is Baton Rouge?" asked Salome.

"We'll probably be there tomorrow," answered Solomon.

"I know you miss your sisters, but how you gonna find them, and how y'all gonna get somewhere where the law won't find you?" asked Mosa.

"I don't know where else to go, and I can't just abandon them. Lord knows who's got them and is probably mistreating them."

Mosa reached out and touched Salome's hand. "Come with me, I've got money at my house. I'm gonna use it to take a boat to New York where my son and daughter are. You'd be safe up there. We could pay someone to find your sisters and arrange for them to join you."

"Really? Do you think that'd work?"

"Definitely."

Salome threw her arms around Mosa.

Later, Mosa sought to engage Solomon in conversation. "You don't talk much."

"No, I'm content with my own company. It's another reason life on the river suits me."

Mosa took the hint. He was doubtless looking forward to having his raft back to himself.

Their trip down the Mississippi was uneventful,

a slow but restful progress where the horrors of Angola receded while the river gently lapped against the raft. Mosa had never spent so long sitting and doing nothing. It was an unknown pleasure to relax and watch the world drift past.

She soon adjusted to the soporific pace. Mosa was in no hurry for the journey to end. Out here she could just be. Be part of nature and let it renew her. Temporarily she was free, free from the tyranny of constant worry of what the day might bring.

When, after a few days, Solomon announced they were as far as he was going, Mosa was jolted back to reality. The raft had been a sanctuary. Stepping onto land that evening and leaving her watery refuge behind knotted Mosa's stomach with a fear she had to fight hard not to show.

CHAPTER 15

Mosa and Salome stayed close to the Backswamp. A full moon lit their way but they kept to the shadows, worried somebody might see them. Out after dark, white folks would automatically assume they were up to no good,.

Mosa was relieved when they reached the house but it was a short lived relief when she remembered she'd have to cross the city in broad daylight to inquire about sailings and buy tickets. Samuel had said to get in touch if she ever needed anything but she couldn't involve him and risk ruining his career. No, she'd have to do it herself and hope. Hope nobody recognized her.

That night she slept in her own bed but home it was no longer. Her children had made it a home. Mosa thought she'd found peace in Tremé, her wanderings finally at end when they arrived in the Crescent City several years ago. But circumstance was pushing her away, leaving her homeless and rootless once more.

The sun was already streaming through gaps between the wooden planks when a noise awoke her. Salome was still sleeping. When the door opened, Mosa's heart accelerated and she jumped out of bed.

The intruder was equally surprised. "Mosa?"

"Angelique!" The two women embraced."

"How - and who's that?" Salome awoke from her slumber, alarm in her eyes.

"There's no need to worry, this here's Angelique, an old friend." Mosa explained to Angelique how they'd come to be here and her plan.

"You're not safe. 'Wanted for murder'. Your face is posted all over the city."

Mosa's legs became paper and she sat on a dining chair and pushed her fingers through her hair. "Gee, I hadn't expected that. Are they offering a reward?"

"Yeah, five hundred dollars. We gotta hope nobody saw you. It's way too dangerous for you to go down to the port to ask about sailings. I'll do it for you. By the way, I got a letter from Thomas. Maisie made it safely to New York. I'll bring it round so you've got the address."

Mosa and Salome spent the day in a tense and fearful silence, whispering when they needed to speak. They could hear the music of life only feet away. People talking and laughing, children playing. A few weeks ago Mosa had been part of that, greeting friends and neighbors while she walked to school to do a job she loved. Now it was a world she was shut out of, a world that mustn't know she was here.

Angelique returned late afternoon with news and a basket of food. "There's no boat to New York, but one's leaving at midnight for England and calling at Charleston. You should be able to pick up a ship to New York from there. We'll take a cab from Congo Square."

"It'll put you at risk, there's no need for you to come along." said Mosa.

"Yes there is. If you speak to the man, he might recognize you and want to claim the reward."

"So might the man checking our tickets when we board."

"Possibly, but he'll most likely be from out of town and not have seen any of those 'wanted' posters. I'm gonna see you get down there safely, you can't stop me."

"Oh Angelique, how I'm gonna miss you."

"Me too, but you must never write in case they intercept-". Angelique's voice faltered. Mosa hugged her while they both cried. That they couldn't at least correspond was too cruel.

Once night fell they emerged from the house, heads bowed. Despite the warmth of the air, shivers ran down Mosa's spine. She and Salome hung back while Angelique spoke to the driver. From the anonymity of the carriage, Mosa watched New Orleans pass by for the last time. Tonight she would either be sailing away or back in jail awaiting the inevitable.

She and Angelique said their goodbyes before Mosa

and Salome got out. In a moment, the carriage had departed and dear Angelique was gone from her life like so many before her. Mosa yearned for a place she would never have to leave and where she could live out her life in peace but it seemed a vain hope, one which had always been denied her.

The ship was a freighter. It carried few passengers. As Angelique had predicted, the man controlling entry was a member of crew and completely unaware of the fact they were fugitives.

Their cabin was small but a welcome cocoon after being in a city which wanted to see them swinging from a rope. When the ship pulled away they exchanged smiles of relief.

For most of the voyage they stayed in their room, emerging only to visit the bathroom and the kitchen to collect their meals. They'd eaten their first meal in the same room as the crew but the long, intrusive stares created an uncomfortable atmosphere.

The vastness of the ocean unsettled Salome. "I don't like all this swaying and not being able to see land. What if we sink? I can't swim."

"Whatever put such a notion in your head? We ain't gonna sink."

To distract her, Mosa produced paper and a pencil from her bag. "I reckon by the time we get to New York, you'll be an excellent reader and writer."

Salome smiled at the thought only briefly, her mind was elsewhere. "How soon do you think we'll be able to get someone to find my sisters?"

"We'll need to get ourselves set up first. I don't want to be a burden on my son. Once we've a place to live, got jobs, and money coming in, it'll be our first priority, I promise."

Arriving in Charleston brought back memories for Mosa of the first time she had journeyed to New York. She recalled the sadness of leaving her brother, Thomas. Her eyes welled while she remembered him waving goodbye, alone and smiling stoically. She didn't know then it was the last time she would ever see him.

Mosa and Salome spent a night in the black part of town and boarded a boat for New York the next afternoon. This time they were required to remain in their cabin. The passenger ship was segregated and the public areas were 'whites only'.

While evening became night on their second day at sea a storm built, howling like a banshee and smashing enormous waves into the vessel. Sleep was impossible. When the ship lurched violently and appeared on the verge of capsizing, Salome screamed. Mosa grabbed her hand. "It's okay."

But it wasn't. An ominous cracking had Salome squeezing Mosa's hand so tightly that it hurt. Only moments later a tolling bell sounded the need to abandon ship. Mosa led Salome up stairs amongst the throng of other passengers. The deck was already sloping and the rear of the vessel perilously close to being underwater. Crew shouted directions and passengers began climbing into the two lifeboats.

An arm flung out created a barrier, stopping Mosa and Salome. "White folks only. You can use that, it'll float." The man pointed to a crate smaller in surface area than a single bed.

"No," protested Mosa, shouting to make herself heard above the wind, "we need to get on the lifeboat, there's still room."

He pointed his handgun at her. "Get back or I'll have to shoot."

In disbelief, the two women watched the lifeboats lowered into the water without them. A wave from behind broke over Mosa and Salome, knocking them onto the deck and sending them sliding helplessly to the stern of the vessel at an ever increasing speed and into the ocean.

Mosa collided with something solid. She spat out the sea water which had filled her mouth. A flash of lightning revealed a plank of wood. She held it with one arm and with the other reached out for Salome's flailing arms. "Grab this and don't let go."

Frequent streaks of lightning illuminated towering waves coming straight at them. Mosa expected the waves to crash down upon them and bring certain death. But each one passed beneath them, raising them high before dropping them into a deep trough. Both were too terrified to speak, grimly clinging on to the plank.

For what seemed like hours the waves kept coming, relentlessly, one after another. Mosa's mouth tasted as if she'd swallowed a cup full of salt and her hands ached from gripping the plank. Her dress was heavy, an anchor eager to plumb the watery depths. She wondered why God had let her escape from Angola only to perish out here.

Yet the storm passed and the surface calmed until it was almost flat. Daybreak revealed coastline on the horizon. Washed up on a sandy beach, they lay supine, spent but grateful. Unable to believe they had survived, they soon fell into a deep sleep of exhaustion.

CHAPTER 16

"Are you all right?" A woman's voice woke them.

"We were shipwrecked," spluttered Mosa, expelling sand from her mouth and squinting in the bright sunshine.

"That figures 'cos you sure don't look like mermaids." The old woman chuckled at her own humor. "Name's Edith. Come with me." Dressed in black and with only two front teeth remaining, her eyes still sparkled with an appetite for life. She led them to her shack. The wood was dark with age and her home looked as precarious as those in Tremé. "I live here alone since my husband died so I got me plenty of room."

Edith took the blankets from her bed. "Take your clothes off and wrap yourself in these. I'll fix you something to eat and then go wash your clothes in the river."

Mosa took off her dress and turned it inside out. When she reached inside the pockets she'd sown there her lips quivered. Only a few soggy dollars remained. "The money I had… it's been washed away, all gone. All those years of work for

nothing." She choked on a sob.
"Where were you headed?" asked Edith.
"New York."
"Ain't never been there, ain't been nowhere other than here."
"Where are we?" asked Mosa.
"Near Wilmington, North Carolina. You're in a good place. At the last elections, we won control of the city government along with the Fusionists - white folks who support us having equal rights."
"Is there work to be had?"
"I dare say but it's gotta be four or five miles from here into town."
"We're used to walking."
Edith's tumbledown dwelling was in sight and sound of the ocean. Mosa could barely bring herself to look at it, but she couldn't block out the ceaseless sound of waves hitting the shore. Like Salome, she too was now terrified by the ocean, that limitless expanse which held you at its mercy. Mosa was haunted by nightmares she was back out there. In her dreams she sank below the surface, the daylight above growing fainter and more distant while her clothes pulled her deeper, and the immense wall of water above her became ever taller. Her nose and mouth filled with sea. Bedtime became a time of dread rather than relaxation.

Salome found work cleaning and Mosa made money giving private tuition. Many black owned businesses prospered in Wilmington, and the owners employed her services to educate their children.

Edith had been right, it was a unique place where there were black policemen, firemen, and magistrates. The city also had its own black-owned newspaper, 'The Daily Record'.

The walk into town from Edith's place soon proved too much. The two of them found lodgings in a house owned by Alex Manly, the editor. He lived in another part of town and they rarely saw him.

Light skinned like Mosa, Alex was the son of a slave and Governor Charles Manly of Raleigh. Alex Manly had taken the paper from a weekly to a daily one.

"We'll stay until next year to rebuild our funds," Mosa told Salome. Mosa felt secure in Wilmington, a rare place where their race wasn't an issue. In a remarkable feat, a black-white coalition had won every state-wide office, including the Governorship at the last elections.

Yet the summer they were there, the atmosphere turned ugly. The safety Mosa thought she'd found turned out to be an illusion. With new state elections looming, white supremacists mounted a ruthless campaign of lies to seize power. They employed their familiar tactic of violence and intimidation to achieve their goal.

"It's exactly what they've done in every other State I ever lived in," commented Mosa to Salome while they sat on the stoop one evening flicking away mosquitoes.

"But I heard tell these are the State elections, there's no election this year for the city government, and we'll be gone by then."

"That's so but Alex Manly is pouring fuel on their fire." Mosa picked up the newspaper on her lap. "Listen to his editorial condemning a Georgia socialite advocating lynching to protect white women. He starts by saying that they make out Negroes are the only criminals."

"What's wrong with that? Many more black women are raped by white men than white women by black men."

"I agree," said Mosa, "but listen to this."

"Every Negro lynched is called a "big burly, black brute," when in fact many of those who have thus been dealt with had white men for their fathers, and were not only not "black" and "burly" but were sufficiently attractive for white girls of culture and refinement to fall in love with them as is very well known to all.

Teach your men purity. Let virtue be something more than an excuse for them to intimidate and torture a helpless people. Tell your men that it is no worse for a black man to be intimate with a white woman than for the white man to be intimate with a colored woman."

"He's speaking the truth," said Salome. "If a white woman gets caught having an affair with a black man, of course she'll cry rape or she'll be driven out of town in disgrace."

"Yes, he's right but most white folks hate the truth, and this kind of language is a gift to those intent on persuading them that we're a threat and should be excluded from voting."

"So we're just expected to shut up and accept their lies? If we do that, nothing's ever gonna change."

Mosa didn't respond, she couldn't argue with that.

That November on election day Mosa shuddered when she saw Red Shirts patrolling the streets with rifles to prevent black people from voting. It brought back memories she didn't want to recall. The awful night when the Red Shirts had marched into her husband's campaign meeting and assassinated him.

All over North Carolina the same occurred to prevent a fair election, resulting in the Democrats taking every seat in the State legislature. Come evening, disturbing news swept across town like a fast spreading wildfire. Hundreds of white citizens were gathering at the court house where 'the White Declaration of Independence' was read out, their leader declaring they would no longer be ruled by men of African origin.

"We should stay here tomorrow and not go outside," said Mosa.

The next morning through a window they observed a mob of armed men going along the street to the office of the 'Daily Record'. They promptly set it alight, cheering as the fire took hold and destroyed the voice of the black population. They then turned their attention to attacking black-owned businesses, shooting residents down while they ran to get away.

"We need to go out the back," said Mosa. Taking Salome's hand, they joined others fleeing into the forest and swamps. They crouched down amongst the dense reeds while raucous birds screeched overhead as if calling out their location.

It was as though they'd gone back in time. Mosa felt yet again like the slave she had been, hiding from a vengeful master. This time death, rather than a whipping, seemed a likely outcome if caught.

Word reached them later in the day that Alex Manly and his brother had fled town and that the marauders had marched to City Hall where they'd forced the resignation of the elected local government at gunpoint. Victory achieved, the white supremacists ceased their rampage and the noise of gunfire ended.

The following day, wet, cold, and wretched, black citizens emerged cautiously from hiding and walked past the smoldering remains of their once happy lives while they headed toward the station. With satisfied smirks on their faces, the insurrectionists watched the black population leave.

Mosa and Salome went with them. It had become too dangerous to remain. Despite not wishing to be a burden, Mosa realized she had no alternative but to ask her son to take them in until they could find work.

"Keep your head down, don't look at nobody and give them a reason to shoot you," said Mosa.

They didn't need to raise their heads to sense the tension. A spark which needed only the slightest of provocations to become flames of murder, and for which those responsible would never be held accountable, exactly as they wouldn't be for yesterday's killings.

America's first coup had taken place. Like the numerous other massacres of African Americans elsewhere in the country, it would be airbrushed from history until late in the twentieth century.

CHAPTER 17

After three days of travel and several changes of train, Mosa and Salome arrived at the Pennsylvania Railroad Station in New Jersey opposite Manhattan, tired but delighted to have made it. Mosa knew that New York wouldn't guarantee their safety, nowhere would. But at least she'd be reunited with her family, which was the most important thing of all. Cruel fate had finally relented and happier times were calling.

They boarded the ferry for the short crossing of the Hudson River. Mosa stood at the bow, welcoming the fresh breeze on her face after so much time in crowded railway cars.

America's largest city was even busier than she remembered it. In the years since she'd left, Manhattan's population had doubled to nearly one and a half million.

When they disembarked, Salome's eyes looked as if they might pop out. She stood and stared, amazed by the crowds and the sight of so many buildings, seemingly endless streets of them. Mosa had to pull her along by the hand like a child to keep her moving.

Mosa too came to a halt when they turned a corner and for the first time saw the 'El', the city's elevated railway system. Up above them, a steam train belched acrid smoke while it pulled two cars. The track, supported by iron girders, kept the sidewalk in gloomy shadow. It was loud and noxious but a wonder nonetheless, a vision of the future.

"Trains in the sky, it's incredible," exclaimed Salome.

On the other side of the street ran the elevated track for trains going in the opposite direction, and in between the two at ground level motorized trams followed tram lines in the pavement. Horses and their carriages, which had once made crossing the city streets hazardous, were much fewer in number than when Mosa had first lived in New York.

"Where are all the colored folks?" asked Salome while they walked. "I've barely seen a black face since we stepped off the ferry."

"It ain't like New Orleans, we're a small minority up here."

They made their way to Little Africa in Greenwich village where much of Manhattan's black population lived, albeit less than two percent of Manhattan's population was then black. It would be another generation until the mass migration from the South began in earnest.

The apartment where Thomas and his family lived was in a brownstone row house. The building was accessed by steps leading to a sturdy front door. Mosa was impressed. This was a solid home, unlike the flimsy houses of Tremé which would collapse like a pack of cards if hit by a hurricane.

Inside, however, appearances were less promising. Wallpaper peeled from the walls revealing mold, and the wooden floors hadn't been varnished in years.

But none of that mattered to Mosa, she was only seconds away from ending years of separation. She hitched her dress up off the ground with her hands and eagerly climbed the staircase, checking numbers on doors as she went. It wasn't until they reached the top floor, she found it. From inside she heard children's voices. Enthusiastically, she knocked.

"I'm Mosa, Thomas's mother," she announced in response to the woman's bewildered look.

"I thought-"

"We got out."

"We?"

Salome stepped forward. "I'm Salome."

"I'm Harriet. You best come in." Thomas's wife's barely suppressed scowl told them she wasn't pleased to have visitors. No longer the radiant bride from the photograph, she appeared weary and harassed, her brown skirt and cream blouse stained with the telltale signs of motherhood.

The room was small. A table and chairs were set against the wall at one end and a mattress occupied most of the remaining space. The window gave a view of the unkept rear of buildings in the adjacent street. In one corner of the room, Mosa could see a door leading to a bedroom.

"We have to share a kitchen and a bathroom one floor down," said Harriet noticing her mother-in-law's rotating neck while she observed her son's home.

"Is Thomas not in?"

"He's not home from work yet and Maisie's at college, that's why I have Josephine."

Two young boys eyed the visitors with suspicion while Josephine crawled along the floor, chuckling while she did so.

"I'm your grandma," beamed Mosa.

The two boys pulled back from the open arms she offered them.

"Joshua and Nate, say hello," demanded Harriet.

Reluctantly they approached Mosa and let her give them a hug.

"What's that mark on your face?" asked Joshua with the innocent curiosity of a child.

"Joshua!" His mother reprimanded him.

"That's okay," said Mosa. "I like that you're observant. I got burned many years ago."

"How?"

"It was an accident." Mosa didn't want to give her grandsons nightmares by telling the truth of how she had been branded with a red hot iron when she'd tried to escape from slavery.

"What happened?"

"Joshua, that's quite enough questions," said Harriet.
Hearing footsteps in the corridor outside the boys ran to the door.
"Daddy!" They flung their arms around his thighs. He quickly extricated himself to embrace his mother.
"It's so good to see you. Maisie told us what you did. How come they let you out?"
Mosa told him of their escape but didn't mention the killing and asked if they could stay for a while.
Out of the corner of her eye, Mosa saw the lowered eyebrows and angry look Harriet was directing at her husband.
"We'd love to have you stay but we don't have the room. Maisie's right across the street. I'm sure she'll be able to help."
When Maisie returned, she screamed with delight and held her mother close but her joy was short lived.
"My place is tiny, just one room. I can't have her as well."
Salome looked down at the floor in embarrassment.
"We'll just have to manage. It'll only be for a short time," said Mosa. "We'll start looking for work first thing tomorrow and soon find our own place to rent."
Maisie wasn't placated. "So you'd rather rent a place with her than find one for you and I?"
"Well, it looks like you're already set up."

Maisie muttered something under her breath which Mosa didn't catch. The family reunion hadn't turned out to be quite the joyous occasion Mosa had imagined.

The next day Salome and Mosa went off in search of work. After making inquiries, Mosa walked to the nearest station of the El, climbed the metal staircase to the track and waited for a train. It had been so many years, she doubted anyone would remember her.

CHAPTER 18

The train terminated at 129th street in Harlem. Mosa walked the next fourteen blocks to where 143rd intersected Amsterdam Avenue. The happy noise of children playing while they enjoyed recess confirmed she had reached her destination. When Mosa entered the building, a woman accosted her.
"Can I help you?" Her tone wasn't welcoming.
"Yes, I was wondering if I could see the Principal."
"About?"
"When I lived in New York many years ago, I taught at the original orphanage. Now I'm back, I've come to find out if I might do so again."
"Let me see if she's able to see you. Wait here." On her return, the woman led Mosa to the Principal's office door. "You may go in."
The Principal stood up from her chair and let out a shriek of delight. "You haven't changed one bit."
Martha came from behind her desk and the two women hugged. Martha had changed. She'd put on weight but then so had Mosa. It was nature's way.
"I can't believe you've come back, I'm so thrilled. Sit down and tell me what you've been up to."

Mosa gave a short and edited account of her life since leaving New York, omitting reference to the reason Thomas had come to live here, and that she'd spent time at Angola and killed somebody. None of those things seemed likely to assist in her search for employment.

"I'm sorry to hear about your husband but I'm so happy you followed your son to New York and that we get to meet again. As you can see, I haven't done badly myself. We're interviewing for a teaching post right now. The Board would need to meet with you, but of course I'll give you a glowing recommendation. Can you come Thursday evening to meet with them? I'd love to have you working here again."

"Of course. And you, did you ever find your husband and children?"

Martha's cheerful disposition vanished. "I did get news. My husband was killed in the War and both my kids died from disease."

"Oh, I'm so sorry, Martha."

"It's been tough but life goes on. It's over ten years now since I found out. I don't know what I would have done without this place. It gave me a purpose, a reason to go on when there didn't seem any point to being alive."

It struck Mosa how lucky she was in comparison. Her life had been hard but her children were safe and well. She found it hard to sleep that night thinking of the heartache Martha had suffered and which would doubtless accompany her until her dying day.

The interview board consisted of two women and two men, one of whom, Elijah Abernathy, was black.

He appeared older than Mosa with gray hair but also urbane in his suit and high collared shirt. His face was round and his eyes were kind. He gave Mosa a warm smile when she entered.

"I hear from our Principal that you were involved in saving our orphans back in '63 during the Draft Riots. It was a brave thing you both did that terrible day." The others nodded in agreement.

After questioning by all of them, Mosa was asked to wait outside while they conferred. She was confident her past history with the orphanage and Martha's recommendation would allay any doubts they might otherwise have.

It was the white male member of the board who addressed Mosa when they called her back in. "We'd like to offer you the position, though there is one thing."

"What's that?"

"We need you to wear makeup to conceal the scar on your face. It might upset the children and we wouldn't want that."

Martha welcomed her to the school the following Monday.

"Mr Abernathy was most complimentary about you. He's a wealthy man. He has a business supplying black servants to New York's elite. Even better, he's a widower," she winked.

"I'm too old for romance," said Mosa.

"Nonsense."

"And what about you? You're still alone by the look of it. You don't have a wedding band on your finger."

Martha paused for a moment and became pensive. "I'm not alone, I have someone."

"You old devil you," laughed Mosa playfully punching her arm. "What's his name?"

"He's a she."

"Oh," said Mosa in an involuntary high pitched squeak of a voice.

"I knew I shouldn't have told you, you'll think less of me now."

"Don't be silly, of course I don't. Everyone should have the right to love whoever they choose, black or white, man or woman. I'm happy for you. A single life can be lonely."

"I must ask you to keep it a secret. I'd be fired if the Board found out. People don't mind so long as they think we're just two ageing spinsters who share a house for companionship."

"Of course, I'll never breathe a word about it."

Mosa was able to get an advance on her pay and, with Martha as a willing guarantor, secure a two bedroomed apartment in Little Africa. Harlem at the time was almost exclusively white, inhabited mainly by Jewish and Italian immigrants.

Maisie insisted on giving up her studio and joining

Mosa and Salome, though she practically ignored Salome. When Salome found a live in job as a maid, Maisie was delighted.

"At last, we'll be together again, just you and I."

"And Josephine," added Mosa. It had become quite apparent to Mosa that Maisie hadn't become any more maternal. She relied on Harriet to look after the child on weekdays and wanted Mosa to take care of her at weekends to leave Maisie free to do whatever she wished.

Sometimes, mother and daughter would take a walk together.

"New York may not be Paris but it's a whole lot better than New Orleans," said Maisie while she and her mother strolled through Washington Square Park one Sunday afternoon. Josephine tottered happily along beside them holding her grandmother's hand.

"How's college going?" asked Mosa.

"Good, but I'm fast using up the money Augustine Dampierre bribed me with. I can't believe she wouldn't help us when I found her broach. I should have left it there in the dust."

"She certainly was a vengeful woman. I'm at least glad you've been able to put the money to good use. You'll be qualified to teach, and there'll always be a demand for that. How come you never bring books home to study?"

Josephine let go of her grandmother's hand and went ahead of them.

"There's no need. I get done all I need to while I'm

at college, and I can't concentrate at home with Josephine always wanting attention."

"Really? You leave me to keep an eye on her whenever I'm at home."

An ear splitting bawling interrupted their conversation. The little girl had fallen on her face, though she didn't appear to have injured herself. Maisie picked her up and tried to calm her. A white woman came rushing over, her face flushed with righteous indignation.

"I wish I knew who the child's mother was, I'd let her know how neglectful you are, chatting and ignoring the poor girl." She wagged a finger at them. "You should be ashamed of yourself."

"I hate bringing her out," complained Maisie once the woman had gone. "I get mistaken for being the nanny all the time."

Mosa realized she'd forgotten how pale Josephine's skin was, so pale that strangers wouldn't think Maisie was her mother and Mosa her grandmother.

CHAPTER 19

Her head down while she tried unsuccessfully to avoid the raindrops, Mosa almost bumped into the man on the sidewalk outside the school gates.
"I'm so sorry."
"Mrs. Elwood." She recognized the sonorous voice from beneath his umbrella.
It was no coincidence, Elijah had been waiting for her to come out. Since the interview a few weeks ago, he'd thought about her often. "Let me hold this over you, I have a hat to keep the rain off."
"Thank you."
"Where are you going?"
"129th, to take the El home."
"Then please let me come with you to keep you dry."
Mosa detected a pleasant smell of lavender accompanying them. She concluded it must be from a balm he applied after shaving.
"How are you finding the school? Is it very different to before?"
"The building's not as nice as the one the rioters burned down but I'm enjoying teaching again.

Children are still children. I love interacting with them and watching them learn, giving them a chance to escape the poverty they've been born into."

Mosa did, however, find it different to before. She knew those young faces saw an older woman in the autumn of her life. A grandmotherly figure, not the youthful woman she'd been the first time around.

"I only wish we could keep them longer," said Elijah. "As you know, once they reach twelve they must leave. We try to find places for them to go, but mostly all that's available is indentured servitude on rural farms. The boys work in the fields and the girls in the house. They're obliged to do so for many years without being paid, supposedly to repay the cost of keeping them, but it's really nothing other than exploitation. They rarely get the opportunity to serve as apprentices like white orphans do. I've been able to take a couple into my business and train them. They've become valued employees."

"How did you get involved with the orphanage?" asked Mosa.

"My wife, who passed five years ago, was on the Board. When she knew she was dying, she asked me to continue her work."

"You must miss her."

"I do. And you? I remember you telling us at your interview that you're a widow."

"Yes, for nearly twenty years now. He was a

politician in South Carolina, shot by the Red Shirts."

"I'm sorry, you must have suffered terribly. By the way, I hope you don't think I was involved in asking you to wear makeup. It was the two female members of the Board. They're like our other white benefactors upon who the school relies for most of its income. They want to help but they don't want the past to be acknowledged."

"Exactly. I'm no longer conscious of my scar and rarely think about it these days unless someone mentions it." Mosa stretched out her hand. "It's stopped raining. I'll be fine from here. Thank you again."

Elijah tipped his hat in farewell. "It's been a pleasure."

On the ride home, Mosa suddenly sensed eyes opposite, watching her. She realized she must have been smiling to herself, replaying the encounter in her mind. She stopped smiling but continued remembering.

Elijah possessed a certain charm and sophistication which she found appealing. Her children were grown, and for the first time in a very long while she was free to focus on what she wanted.

Perhaps... Looking down the car her daydreaming came to a screeching halt. She recognized the back of that head. But the woman next to him who he was being so attentive to most definitely wasn't his wife.

They stood when the train approached the stop before Mosa's. She could immediately see by the way they stared into each other's eyes that it was more than friendship. Neither Thomas or Salome noticed Mosa when they passed her seat.

Mosa spent the rest of the day pondering what to do. If she went to confront Thomas at home Harriet would be there, and if Mosa asked for a word alone what would he say to his wife when she asked what his mother had wanted? He'd never been a good liar. Instead, Mosa waited for Salome to visit.

"What's going on between you and Thomas?" demanded Mosa the moment Salome walked in. Maisie's eyes widened with interest at this unexpected news.

"Nothing," answered Salome, but she didn't look at Mosa when she spoke.

"It sure didn't look like nothing when I saw the two of you riding the El the other day."

"We bumped into each other."

Arms crossed, Mosa sharpened her tone. "Don't lie to me, I risked my life for you. Is this how you repay me?"

"But he's not happy."

"His happiness isn't your concern. I expect you to end whatever it is immediately."

"You don't understand-"

"There's nothing to understand, other than what I've just said. Do you understand that?"

Sheepishly, Salome nodded.

"Good, we'll talk no more about it. Now come sit down."

Tears escaped and ran down Salome's cheeks. "I need to go." She hurried out of the apartment.

"What was that all about?" asked Maisie, unable to disguise her glee that Salome's friendship with her mother might be at an end.

"You heard, and you'll say nothing to nobody."

There was another matter bothering Mosa so she decided to investigate. She visited the college.

"We have no one enrolled here by that name."

"Maybe she's enrolled by another name - Dampierre perhaps?"

The clerk ran his finger down the register and shook his head.

A mild fall day persuaded Mosa to give her the benefit of the doubt and wait outside for classes to finish. She watched the students leave, waiting for her to appear.

That evening, once Josephine was asleep Mosa challenged her daughter.

"Why are you lying to me about going to college?"

"I don't know what you mean."

"I wasn't born yesterday, Maisie. They have no record of you, and I saw the students leave and you weren't one of them. Just what is it you get up to every day?" Maisie failed to respond. "Well?"

"I'm learning French."

Mosa sighed with irritation. "Surely you're still not

thinking about going to Paris."

"Why not? Why shouldn't I be able to follow my dream?" protested Maisie. "New York ain't that different to New Orleans, look at all the stores and other places we can't go in. The housing's segregated, and the schools too. I hate always being at the bottom, looked down upon. Is that what you want for me?"

"You know what I want for you, a reliable job so that you and Josephine will have a stable future. You need to pull your head down out of the clouds."

"And have the life you've had? No thanks."

Mosa's anger boiled over. Without thinking, she slapped Maisie's face. For a moment both were speechless, each shocked by what had happened.

"I'm going out." Maisie grabbed her coat and left, slamming the door behind her as she went.

Stressed, Mosa sat down and rubbed her palm repeatedly against her forehead. She fretted that Maisie's behavior was her fault, that she had failed to raise her daughter properly.

CHAPTER 20

Later that same evening, Thomas appeared at Mosa's door, his expression glum.

"Harriet's kicked me out. Can I stay here tonight? Maisie says she's gonna stay with Harriet and you can drop Josephine there in the morning."

"Oh did she. How did Harriet find out?"

"I don't know, but - wait a minute, how do you know? Did you tell her?"

"No, but I saw you and Salome on the El. It needs to end, you have responsibilities to your family."

Thomas sat down on a dining chair and pushed his fingers through his hair. "You don't know how hard it is, working in the warehouse all day and playing in a band at night, and we're still barely surviving. I need some joy in my life."

"Don't you tell me I don't know how hard it is. You ain't been whipped and got the scars on your back as a constant reminder or branded on the face with a hot iron. Nor have you been a slave or had to bring up two children on your own. You and your sister don't know how lucky you are. So quit moaning and start being a man. I'm off to bed."

Mosa was still fuming when she traveled to work the next morning. Snapping at the children in class, she realized her mood hadn't improved.

"What do you want?" She was curt even with Elijah when she saw him waiting outside the school again.

"Sounds like now might not be a good time."

"I've had a bad day."

"Well, I was kind of hoping what I have to ask might cheer you up. I was wondering if you might like to come for lunch this Saturday."

A maid opened the door at the house a couple of blocks back from Central Park. It was a world Mosa had experienced when in Bath, England, and then she had done so as an employee not a guest. A secret world behind closed doors, a world that was abundant and sumptuous.

"I'm so glad you came, what do you think of the house?" asked Elijah.

"I love it," said Mosa surveying the fine art on the walls and elegant furniture, all a far cry from the apartment where she lived without luxuries of any sort.

"I wanted to buy one overlooking Central Park but they didn't like the color of my money, or rather my skin. I may be a successful entrepreneur but it's still not enough for those who get to decide who lives where."

Lunch was served on bone china at a long mahogany table. Elijah sat opposite her rather than occupying the head of the table where Mosa expected he usually ate his meals. She appreciated the gesture.

Afterward, he suggested they visit the Metropolitan Museum of Art.

"When I was first in New York, they were busy constructing Central Park and now look at it, trees that are tall, and a museum as big as a King's palace," commented Mosa as they approached the building.

"Why did you leave?" asked Elijah.

"It's a long story, for another day. Let's go see ourselves some art."

The couple met every weekend after that. Elijah took Mosa to see other changes in the city since she had first lived here. Walking across the recently constructed Brooklyn Bridge and its spider's web of cables above them, Mosa slipped her arm through his. It seemed the right thing to do. She wanted him to know she liked him and was happy in his company.

"Were you ever a slave?" asked Mosa.

"No, fortunately I was born and raised in New York after 1827 when it had ended. However, my parents were as good as slaves for half of their lives. When slavery was supposedly abolished in the State in 1799, it didn't free a single person. Only those born later weren't considered to be slaves, and even then they had to work for their mother's master without payment until they were in their late twenties. You gotta hand it to white folks, they're as cunning as foxes in looking after their own interests."

"That they sure are," agreed Mosa. "Now they throw us in jail for the slightest reason so we can be hired out to work for nothing while the prison owners make a fortune from keeping the money they make from that."

A few days before Christmas, Elijah took Mosa on a sleigh ride through Central Park. The cold stung her cheeks but she enjoyed how bracing the air was. She hadn't seen snow like this since leaving New York. The winter sunshine made it sparkle, and bells tied to the horses complimented the swoosh of the sleigh to create a magical experience.

When Elijah produced a small red box from his coat pocket, Mosa's heart swelled.

For days, Mosa floated on clouds. Martha grabbed her hands and spun her around her with joy when Mosa told her Elijah had proposed.

"Stop, you're making me dizzy," laughed Mosa. "I haven't said yes yet."

"Why ever not?"

"I'm considering it."

"Do you love him?"

"Yes, I believe I do."

"Then don't hesitate, none of us are getting any younger. This is your time for happiness. You deserve this, don't let it slip through your fingers."

Mosa didn't tell her friend her hesitation wasn't because of Elijah.

The following day, her heart turned over when she knocked on his front door. In a few minutes she would have her answer.

Elijah turned from looking out of the window when Mosa was shown into his study. He appeared nervous.

"I would love to marry you." Elijah exhaled with relief and came toward Mosa his arms outstretched but Mosa raised a hand. "There's something you don't know about me. If what I'm about to tell you makes you want to withdraw your proposal I shall completely understand, and I release you from any obligation you might feel you have toward me."

Elijah listened in silence until she'd finished. "It changes nothing. You were innocent, and killing the prison guard was totally justified." He reached inside his jacket pocket and slipped the ring he'd shown her a few days earlier onto her finger.

"Are you sure?"

"I ain't ever been more sure of anything in my life." Elijah pulled her close for a kiss.

"Isn't it time to show me the upstairs?" laughed Mosa.

Mosa grinned all the way home. All those years of hurt and struggle were over. All those nights she'd cried herself to sleep were behind her. Even when she slipped on ice on the sidewalk and landed on her rear, she chuckled.

Thomas was back with Harriet, Maisie had agreed to start college in September, and all was right in Mosa's world. She hadn't yet told her children about Elijah's proposal. It had all happened so fast but she was sure they'd be happy for her.

When she reached the apartment, she was surprised to find Maisie and Josephine weren't there. Taking off her fur hat, she laid it on the table. It was only then that she noticed the letter addressed to her.

CHAPTER 21

Mosa read the letter with increasing disbelief.

I'm sorry to disappoint you but I have to follow my dream. I know many will vilify me, a mother abandoning her daughter, yet men do it all the time and few think the worse of them because of it.
I hope with time you will come to forgive me.
I need to be free, truly free, and find a freedom that doesn't exist for us in America.
Josephine adores you and it'll be better for her to grow up with you than with a mother who can't give her the love and attention you will.
I'll write once I get to Paris.
PS I've left Josephine at Harriet's

Mosa slumped into a dining chair. How could it be that each time her life seemed to take a turn for the better, something would always come along and derail her plans? Mosa didn't welcome the prospect of being responsible for her granddaughter but she had no choice. The child needed the love she'd give her more than ever now.

But there was also someone else to consider. Elijah

knew her daughter had a young child, but what would he think about living with her? He'd never had children of his own, and how many men of nearly sixty years of age would want a youngster to raise, especially one they weren't the father of?

Maisie stood on deck while Manhattan grew smaller as the ship sailed past the gigantic, robed Roman goddess holding a torch above her head in her right hand and a tablet in her left. At her feet lay a broken shackle and chain, symbolizing freedom from oppression and liberty. Standing on a pedestal, she was the tallest thing in the city, a copper colossus which hadn't yet acquired a green patina from oxidization. Gustave Eiffel, the creator of the famous tower in Paris, had been involved in constructing this gift from France.

Magnificent though the the Statue of Liberty undoubtedly was, Maisie recalled an article she'd read in a black-owned newspaper, which encapsulated well her reason for seeking freedom elsewhere.

"Liberty enlightening the world," indeed! Shove the statue, torch and all, into the ocean until the "liberty" of this country is such as to make it possible for an inoffensive and industrious colored man to earn a respectable living for himself and family, without being ku-kluxed, perhaps murdered, his daughter and wife outraged, and his property destroyed. The idea of the "liberty" of this country "enlightening the world" is ridiculous in the extreme."

Maisie harbored no doubts. She was certain she had made the right decision.

"We need to talk." Mosa delivered the words abruptly immediately the maid who had showed her in departed.

"That sounds rather ominous," said Elijah, rising from his chair. "Please don't tell me you've changed your mind."

"No, but I got home last night to discover Maisie has left and gone to Paris to live."

"I remember you saying she wanted to."

"Yes, but I thought she'd let that go."

"Your children are both grown, Mosa. They're gonna go down the path they choose whether you like it or not."

"That's not the issue. She left Josephine behind, with me."

"Oh." Elijah stroked his chin in contemplation.

"I must put the needs of Josephine first, and I can't expect you to take on my granddaughter. I'm sorry, Elijah."

"I must admit it's not something I'd have chosen, but if my choices are to lose you or to take your granddaughter as well, it's any easy decision. Though may I suggest we hire a nanny so we'll still have time to ourselves?"

Mosa threw her arms around him. "Of course, and thank you."

"You don't have any other surprises for me, do you?"

"No."

"Good. Now, what would you like for a wedding gift? A nice piece of jewelry, perhaps?"

Mosa only had to think for a moment. "There is something I'd like you to do for me, though it doesn't involve jewelry."

Their wedding took place at City Hall, a glorious wedding cake of a building with its Corinthian columns, arched windows, marble facade, and a domed tower. Save for the absence of Maisie, it was a perfect day. Mosa dressed in bright blue reflecting the cloudless winter sky outside and wore a white fur cloak for warmth.

The night before she'd struggled to sleep, tossing and turning until almost dawn. Mosa believed she was doing the right thing but she was troubled nonetheless. Surely no man could be so virtuous as Elijah appeared to be. Was he really a man with no vices or was he skilled at hiding his? Would she discover something that would burst her balloon of happiness? After so many years of independence, could she unwittingly be making a mistake?

Escorted by her son, Mosa entered the building and ascended one side of the double curved staircase beneath the spectacular rotunda. She dismissed the last lingering doubt and allowed herself to feel special to a degree she couldn't recall ever having done so.

Elijah looked handsome in his new suit bought for

the occasion. He had told Mosa to spend whatever she needed to so she had taken Harriet shopping to get her a new dress to wear. Mosa was pleased to note that even her normally rather sullen daughter-in-law was smiling that day. Pleased no doubt for once to feel good about how she looked, and enjoying a rare day off from housework and cooking.

The newly wed couple honeymooned at Niagara. Partially frozen like a scene from a fairy tale, the Falls were a thing of wonder, nature at her harshest yet most beguiling. In the mornings, they took brisk walks and romantic sleigh rides, and in the afternoons they read in front of the roaring log fire in their suite and drank hot cocoa. At night, they renewed their souls wrapped in each other's arms.

Once back in the city, Mosa soon became accustomed to being mistress of the house and letting servants do the daily chores. She acquiesced in Elijah's request she give up working and took his place on the board of the orphanage.

Elijah arranged for Thomas and his family to move to a two bedroomed apartment with its own kitchen and bathroom. Mosa's heart overflowed with love and gratitude when Elijah told her what he'd done. He was indeed a very special man; kind, caring, and generous.

Maisie wrote rarely and said little when she did. She gave no address other than a 'poste restante'. She sent her love for Josephine but didn't inquire how she was.

Mosa's heart ached for the child, she too had had a mother who didn't care. It was a hurt that went deep, a hurt that never really went away. Elijah spent most weekdays at his office so for a great deal of the time Mosa was able to relieve the nanny and take care of her granddaughter and give her the love and attention which had been lacking in Mosa's childhood.

It was when spring flowers reclaimed Central Park from the bone chilling grip of winter that Mosa's wedding gift from Elijah bore fruit.

CHAPTER 22

"I received a visit today from the private detective agency I hired," announced Elijah while they ate dinner. "They've been found."

The following day Mosa went to visit her. She was surprised to see Mosa. It was the first time since Mosa had told Salome to stay away from Thomas. She'd never been back to Mosa's apartment after that and had never expected Mosa to contact her again.

"Can I come in?"

Salome didn't open the door any wider, still only revealing half her face. "Not really, the owner will be home soon, and she wouldn't take kindly to me inviting people in."

"It's about your sisters. I know where they are."

Salome's dour expression brightened. "You better step inside."

"I met a kind man, he's my husband now, and he arranged for someone to go look for them."

"Oh my." Salome's eyes became rheumy. "I thought after…you know, that you'd never want anything to do with me again."

"I made a promise, I promised you we'd find them."
"Where are they?"
"They're still in Baton Rouge. The district attorney took them in and has them working in his house."
Salome sighed. "He's a mean one, the same man who prosecuted me, and now he gets to profit from sending me to jail. I need to go fetch them."
"There's no need, Elijah will get someone to bring them."
"That won't work, they'll be too frightened to run off with a stranger. They're both under ten."
"If you went, you'd risk being caught and hung," objected Mosa.
"I'll be careful. It's a risk I'm willing to take. They're all I have left in this world. Life without them is too hard." Salome forced an end to their encounter. "Thank you so much for what you've done. I'll always be grateful but I'm gonna have to ask you to leave, Mrs. Jordan will be back any minute."
Walking back home, anxiety wound itself around Mosa like a noose. If Salome was apprehended that would be bad enough, but that wasn't where it would end. They'd interrogate her, beat her up, maybe offer her a plea bargain, whatever it took until she told them. Told them where Mosa was.
A request for extradition would be made. The New York authorities would have to comply. It was the law. Mosa would be arrested and sent back to Louisiana in chains to be hung after a show trial that would ignore the fact she'd been defending a young woman who was being raped.

"We have to stop her," said Elijah when Mosa told him that evening of Salome's plan.

"How? She's determined to go."

"I have people who can take care of her while I get someone down there to bring them back."

Mosa didn't like what she heard. "What do you mean by that? You can't kidnap her."

"She'll be kept in comfort." He failed to deny that she'd be held against her will. "We must stop her being a danger to herself and, more importantly, to you."

Mosa bit her nails. Her worry intensified the next day when Elijah got home, his usual smile at seeing his wife absent.

"It's too late, she's already left. I'll send someone after her but he's unlikely to catch up with her. She probably went yesterday."

Mosa put her hand on the credenza to steady herself. How naive she had been to think she'd finally managed to outrun her past.

In the days which followed Mosa lost her appetite and slept little. At each knock on the front door she became rigid, imagining that blue hat and cape and handcuffs dangling from his hand.

"You should go visit Maisie, take Josephine to see her mother. I'll send word as soon as there's news," urged Elijah.

"But what about you?"

"I'll miss you, of course, but your freedom is the most important thing."

A telegram was sent to the 'post restante' address to inform Maisie where Mosa would be staying.

In Baton Rouge, Salome crouched behind bushes, impatiently waiting for evening to surrender to night. Her blouse was damp from the sweat of fear. The journey down had lasted several days. Salome was convinced her backside would be permanently indented from sitting for so long on the slatted wooden benches in the cars black folks had to use.

The closer she'd got to Louisiana, the more her anxiety had grown, hanging in the air all around her like a malevolent phantom who refused to give her a moment's peace, telling her she'd never get away with it. Arriving late afternoon, she'd hurried from the station, head down, worried somebody might recognize her.

When the last light went out in the large house opposite, she broke cover and went around the back of the property, her mouth dry and her temples pulsating so much she could hear it. Slowly she turned the handle to the back door. Thankful to find it wasn't locked, she gently eased it open, ready to run if they had a hound whose bark would rouse the owners.

Entering the kitchen, the different shades of the shadows revealed a crumpled heap in one corner, two small sleeping bodies lying together under a shared blanket. Salome's heart filled with love. In their sleep, her two sisters held each other for comfort. Fallen angels made to sleep where they worked, robbed of childhood and play. Denied an education, their destiny was set to be one of servitude with no chance of improving their prospects.

Salome kneeled down beside them and caressed their foreheads to wake them.

"Don't say anything," she whispered. "It's me, your big sis. I've come to take you away from here."

Their small hands tightly gripping hers, Salome led them out and down the side of the house. They'd hide in the fields on the edge of town for the rest of the night and catch the first train out. Salome prayed it would leave before the district attorney and his wife woke up to discover the girls gone.

Without a sound, the three of them crept along the street. When a man appeared from behind a tree and blocked their path, Salome threw her arms around her sisters and pulled them close. She couldn't run. She might get away but they wouldn't.

Mosa experienced no excitement when the horse pulled their cab away from the house and familiarity. Instead, a fog of emptiness swallowed her. She'd spent her life running. Each and every time she thought she'd found home, the comfort and stability it brought had been snatched from under her leaving her vulnerable and frightened. Mosa had never thought she'd still be running at her age and yet she was.

Josephine leaned into her grandmother's side and held her arm, she was too little to understand. Mosa hadn't mentioned they might be seeing her mother, only that they were taking a boat trip. She didn't want Josephine to face disappointment if Maisie failed to show up at their hotel.

New York, a city Mosa had come to love, was slipping away, dispassionate and disinterested that she was leaving. Mosa understood this might well be the last time she ever saw these streets. Worse was the thought she may never again set eyes upon Thomas and his family. Last night when she went to his apartment to tell him, she'd saved her tears until she left, the innocent cries of 'see you soon, grandma' from his two boys ringing in her ears.

Mosa wondered if her marriage might be over before it had barely begun. Elijah was a New Yorker through and through. He'd said he'd come join her if need be but would he? And if he did, how long would he be able to take it, cut off from all he'd ever known?

At the port, Josephine followed Mosa's instructions to keep hold of her hand. The throng of people was frightening, a forest of limbs she'd be hopelessly lost in, unable to find her grandmother should anyone come between them.

Looking up at the huge hull, a wave of nausea hit Mosa and she swayed. After nearly drowning, she'd sworn never to go out on the ocean again.

Mosa inhaled deeply. Steeling herself, she led Josephine toward the gangway. Mosa sought consolation in the thought that this time she wouldn't be confined to a windowless cabin for the voyage. There was no segregation on this French vessel, and they would be traveling first class.

"Stop! Wait!" Mosa froze. Somebody was shouting, and for her, she was certain of it. Mosa quickened her pace, dragging Josephine by the hand and onto the gangway. The ship was French territory. They couldn't arrest her once she was on board.

CHAPTER 23

"Mosa, it's me." Elijah burst through the wall of humanity below. "I have news, wonderful news! My man caught up with Salome. They're on their way back, all of them."

Mosa burst into tears, causing Josephine to do the same. Mosa hugged her. "Everything's fine, honey. Your grandma's crying tears of happiness. We're going back home."

When Salome and her sisters reached New York, they were brought to Elijah's house. The two girls hid their faces in Salome's blouse.

"Would you like lemonade and cookies?" asked Mosa. Both looked out from their refuge and nodded, although their faces remained solemn. "Well, let me take you to meet Josephine, and then Salome and I will go to the kitchen and rustle you up a treat."

"I've been so worried about you," said Mosa while preparing a tray for the girls. She didn't mention fears for her own safety and how she'd almost sailed away across the Atlantic.

"I waited until nightfall and went in through the

back door. They were made to sleep in the kitchen like mousers so I found them straightaway. Although Mr. Jones sure frightened the heck out of me when he appeared out of nowhere."

"I'm happy for you, you have your family back. How will you manage, though?"

"Mrs. Jordan told me she'd have me back but she won't take my sisters, she was quite clear about that. I don't know what to do."

"I'd offer to have them here, but Elijah's already compromised enough by agreeing to have Josephine. I can only push him so far." Suddenly inspired by a thought, she raised her right index finger in the air. "I might be able to get them in at the orphanage, they are orphans after all, and that way they'd also get an education."

Salome's face became sunshine. "Really? That would be wonderful."

Mosa's life settled into a pleasant routine of attending meetings of charity boards in the mornings, playing with Josephine in the afternoons, and spending the evenings with Elijah when he made it home before bedtime. Sometimes, it was after midnight when he rolled in but she didn't complain. He worked so very hard and for such long hours. That he met up with friends didn't bother her, he deserved some fun. His breath smelled of bourbon but he was never drunk.

For their first married Christmas together, Mosa

decided to take control. She'd never been able to give her family the kind of celebration she would have liked to. Lack of money had always kept it a frugal affair.

For the first time in her life, Mosa embraced extravagance. Large Christmas trees reaching almost to the high ceilings were ordered for both the lounge and dining room, and there were more candles in the house than at a saint's shrine.

Mosa gave the staff the day off so they could spend it with their families and prepared Christmas lunch herself. She invited Martha and her partner, Louise, to join them. Louise wasn't ebullient like Martha but quiet and thoughtful. Mosa considered they complemented each other perfectly.

With Thomas and his family there it was a loud and jolly occasion. Mosa's greatest pleasure was watching her grandchildren opening their gifts from 'Santa Claus' under the tree. Her heart was overflowing as she watched her family in the glow of firelight. All was right with her world, save for only one thing, her absent daughter.

When Martha and Louise announced they must go, Mosa accompanied them to the door.

"I'm so glad to have met you, Louise, and so happy for you both that you found each other."

"Thank you, and for your discretion. Most would shun us if they knew the truth."

"Sadly, yes. But I still live in hope that one day, whenever that might be, we can inhabit a world where race or who we choose to love won't be held against us."

That evening, Mosa wrote to Maisie asking her when she was coming back. Hoping to persuade her, she enclosed a recent photograph of Josephine looking angelic in a white dress and with a white bow in her hair. When her daughter next wrote some months later, she ignored the question.

My French is almost fluent and Paris is all I hoped it would be. I feel so at home and so free. My color isn't an issue. Only once have I encountered the disdain I experienced almost every day in America.
You'll be pleased to know I'm doing well. I give private English lessons and I'm even writing short stories based on my life here. Who knows, maybe one day some publisher will want them.
Glad to hear all is well. Give Josephine a kiss for me.

As Mosa grew older, it seemed to her that the passing of time accelerated. In what felt like the blink of an eye, Josephine had already reached school age.

She asked about her mother infrequently and appeared accepting when Mosa would tell her she was extremely busy and wouldn't be coming home anytime soon. Still, Mosa worried. The child didn't want for love but Mosa knew when the girl grew older, the lack of motherly love would make her feel abandoned and insecure like it had Mosa. And Josephine would face the same challenge of fitting in, if not more so. Her granddaughter's complexion remained as pale as the day she was born.

Questions about what friends she'd made at school were brushed aside but Mosa persisted.

"It's your birthday soon. How about a big party with a magician? All your friends at school can come."

"I don't want a party."

"Why ever not?"

"Because I don't," shouted Josephine running up the stairs to her room.

Going into her bedroom to investigate, Mosa found her granddaughter face down on the bed. Mosa sat down next to her. "Tell me what's wrong, honey."

"You wouldn't understand."

Mosa reached out for her hand. "I think I might. When I was about your age, kids didn't want to play with me because they thought I was too white."

Josephine sat up, her eyes wet. "You're nowhere near as white as me. I hate my color and I hate school. No one will play with me. They say I should leave and go to a white school."

"Come here." Mosa pulled her in for a cuddle. "You know I'm a teacher, don't you? How about if you stayed at home and I taught you?"

Josephine nodded enthusiastically, smiling through her tears. Mosa's pleasure that she'd cheered up her granddaughter didn't last. She knew she was only postponing the problem instead of helping her granddaughter face it head on and learning to live with it.

Each day, unless it was raining, the two of them would visit Central Park in the afternoon after a morning of homeschooling. Mosa hadn't the energy these days to chase her granddaughter so she sat on a bench and let her run around.

It wasn't long before Josephine made a friend to play with, a white girl. The woman keeping an eye on her and seated on a nearby bench was black and clearly the child's nanny. She looked in Mosa's direction and gave a brief incline of the head. Doubtless the woman would be thinking Mosa was also a servant.

At the end of their play, Josephine's cheeks were flushed like a red apple. She skipped happily beside her grandmother while they began the walk home.

"That was Annabelle. She's gonna ask if I can go to their house where we can play with her dolls."

Mosa halted, turning to look at Josephine and taking her hands in hers. "Honey, don't you see what'll happen? Her mother will find out who your family are, and then she won't want Annabelle to see you anymore."

"You don't know that," challenged her granddaughter. "She might not be like that."

"I'm afraid she almost certainly will be, and I don't want to see you get hurt. Hey, how about we get some ice cream?"

"No, I hate my life. My Mama don't want me, other kids don't want me, nobody wants me." Josephine let go of her grandmother's hand and ran ahead. The moment they got back, she went upstairs.

Mosa sat in the living room, thinking. Later that day she went to visit Salome.

"They'd love that. I'll be sure to talk to them beforehand so they don't mention anything about her color."

And so Josephine found friends. They may have been older than her but they were more than happy to oblige. Josephine had better toys than the orphanage had and the food they ate while at the house was so much tastier.

CHAPTER 24

"We need to talk," announced Elijah placing his hat on the stand when he came through the front door. His abruptness and severe expression set Mosa's heart racing. This wasn't the easy going, happy man she knew. "Let's go in the study."

"What is it, Elijah? You're worrying me."

He faced the window, not looking at his wife. "I'm in debt."

"How bad is it?"

"We'll need to get rid of the staff and sell this place."

"I thought business was good, at least that's what you've been telling me. Elijah, look at me."

He turned, his face reflecting shame and embarrassment. "It is but there's something you don't know. You married a gambler. Every week I play poker and I've been having a losing streak, a long one."

"Will the business survive?"

"Just about but our lifestyle won't."

"We'll survive. I've never been that comfortable having people waiting on me, and I miss not teaching. I could go back to it if we need the money."

"It would sure help. I've enough left to get us an apartment. You really are something, Mosa."

"Yes, I certainly am. We married for better or worse so I'll let this go. We all make mistakes." Her tone hardened. "But a mistake isn't a mistake if you keep repeating it. I need you to solemnly promise me that you're done with gambling. Be in no doubt, Elijah, if you break your promise, I'll leave you. I can accept falling on hard times but I won't be made a fool of."

Elijah didn't argue. "I promise, I couldn't bear to lose you."

"Remember that each time you're tempted, because you will be tempted."

That night while Elijah snored, Mosa stared into the darkness, thinking. She'd often wondered what fault he might have. Yet it could have been worse, he could have told her he was having an affair or that he was leaving her. However, she'd need to see if he kept his promise. Mosa loved him but she owed it to herself, and to Josephine too, not to let them be dragged down with him if he wouldn't stop.

Mosa had lived alone before. She didn't want to again but she would if she had to. She refused to be a victim, that wasn't who she was. Mosa sighed. Why did life always seem to kick the ground from under her just when she thought her troubles were behind her.

Despite what she'd said to Elijah she did enjoy her life of privilege, someone to clean the house and wash their clothes and cook their meals. Going back to work would be tough after getting used to an existence of undemanding good deeds and extensive leisure time. But, she told herself, there were many reasons to be grateful. A great many didn't have the blessings she'd still be left with even once the house was no longer theirs.

They took an apartment in Harlem. It was no mansion but it had its own kitchen and bathroom and was only a few years old. They chose Harlem because it was a cheap neighborhood and convenient for teaching at the orphanage. The area also offered easy access to greenery. Fields and forest were nearby. On the outskirts of the city at the time, Harlem was almost bucolic.

Back working full time, Mosa could no longer homeschool Josephine.

"But I don't wanna go to school and have all the kids tease me," she protested.

"I understand but I think I have the answer. Try this." Mosa held out a small round tin. She rubbed some powder from it onto Josephine's hand. "See. It makes your skin darker. We can apply it to your face and hands each morning."

Josephine grunted but she had no choice, and a school for white children wouldn't accept her because of who her family were.

As the last decade of the nineteenth century

drew to a close, Mosa's mortality stared back at her whenever she looked in the mirror. Her hair was mainly gray and the lines around her eyes and mouth were becoming ever more pronounced. Looking down at her hands, she saw the raised veins of old age.

Mosa didn't worry for herself, she'd already lived longer than most. She worried for her granddaughter. Josephine was only ten years old.

Mosa wrote to Maisie urging her to come home for her daughter's sake. It was three months until a reply came.

I know I must disappoint you but I'm not you. I never was and never can be. My life is here in Paris. You should send Josephine to visit me when she's older. I think she'd like it here and could probably make a better life for herself in Paris than New York.

Frustrated, Mosa tore the letter up and threw it on the fire. She put on her hat and coat and went to see Harriet.

"Oh, hello. Thomas isn't in." She and Mosa had never become close, although Mosa had hoped they might.

"That doesn't matter, it's you I came to see," said Mosa stepping forward and obliging Harriet to open the door fully and let her in. "I wanted to talk to you about Josephine."

"What about her?"

"I'll be sixty next year and I worry what'll happen to her if I die."

"You ain't sick, are you?"

"No but I'm getting old. I wrote to Maisie asking her to come home but she won't so I came to ask if you would take care of Josephine if I'm no longer around."

"What about Elijah?"

"He's older than me and not suited to guide a girl of her age if he survives me."

Harriet folded her arms. "I don't mean to be unkind but she has a mother. She needs to take responsibility. If she won't come back then Josephine needs to go to Paris. Was there anything else? I need to get dinner ready."

Mosa didn't press the matter. After all, Harriet was right. It was as Maisie had written, she was a huge disappointment to her mother. Mosa wrote again to Maisie, her letter curt this time.

If anything should happen to me, you'll have no choice but to take care of your daughter. As you refuse to return, she would be sent to Paris to live with you.

That night, Mosa prayed to the Lord to spare her a few more years. Her granddaughter already felt unwanted and with good reason, a mother who'd abandoned her and a father who didn't know she existed. Putting the child on a boat across the ocean when there was no guarantee her mother would step up and look after her hardly seemed a solution to the problem.

CHAPTER 25

On New Year's Eve 1899, it seemed the entire city had come out to celebrate on a crisp and frosty evening. Many blew on their tin horns as had been the custom for several years now. Not everyone appreciated the noise they made.

"What a din," complained Mosa while they sauntered amongst the good natured crowds in Central Park.

"I think it's fun," said Josephine.

"It's a sign we're getting old," added Elijah.

"Speak for yourself," retorted Mosa sharply. She was allowed to think she was getting old but he most certainly wasn't allowed to say so.

At midnight, the bells chimed in the change and then peeled to celebrate.

"A new century." Mosa spoke the words in a tone of disbelief.

"Maybe this one I'll get to see my mother," said Josephine.

Mosa blinked rapidly, forcing back tears. How she felt for her granddaughter, she deserved so much better.

When they got home, Josephine went to bed and Elijah did too. Mosa stayed up, thinking. So much had changed during the last century. Electricity and telephones and trains, and now motor cars had been invented. Yet, on a human level, the attitudes of most people hadn't advanced much, if at all. The freedom Emancipation appeared to promise was down and out, stamped upon by those holding the reins of power.

During Reconstruction, great progress had been made. Mosa had witnessed it with her own eyes. The future had looked brighter and full of hope. For a short while it had really seemed that liberty for all, as supposedly guaranteed by the Constitution, would be upheld. But since the end of Reconstruction, the cause of freedom for anyone who wasn't white had gone into reverse. Mosa didn't expect to live to see equal rights. She could only hope that her granddaughter would.

America claimed to be a democracy, but its elections weren't free and fair. In large swathes of the country, particularly the South, a significant percentage couldn't vote because of their color. That would remain the case until the Civil Rights legislation of the 1960s, a whole one hundred years after Emancipation.

When Elijah arrived home one summer's evening in the first year of the twentieth century with blood on his white shirt, his lip cut, and his left eye almost shut with swelling, Mosa couldn't contain her anger.

"I told you I wouldn't put up with your gambling, Elijah Abernathy. I'm not hanging around to watch loan sharks kill you or wait for them to harm me and Josephine." Elijah walked wearily to a dining chair and sat down. "You promised-"

"I've kept my promise. This ain't what it looks like."

"Just what is it then? Don't you dare say you tripped on the sidewalk."

"There's rioting downtown. The word on the street is one of our guys got into a fight with a police officer who wasn't in uniform and who was harassing his wife. The policeman has died, which has unleashed an outpouring of hatred. When the train stopped, white folks dragged me and the other black folks off and beat us up. Plenty of police were there. They could have intervened but they just stood and watched. If you don't believe me, ask around or read tomorrow's paper."

Mosa placed a hand on his shoulder. "I'm sorry for jumping to conclusions. Stay there and I'll get a washcloth to clean you up."

While she gently dabbed his face, Mosa was seized with worry. "Thomas and his family are probably caught up in it. I need to go down there and check on them."

Elijah grabbed her arm. "Please don't, it's too dangerous. I'll go in the morning."

"No, a man's much more likely to be attacked. I'll go myself, first thing."

An uneasy peace of sullen looks and boarded

windows reigned when Mosa walked through her son's neighborhood.

"You shouldn't have come," said Thomas when he opened the door. "Everyone's staying home. It's not safe out there."

"I had to know if you were all safe," said Mosa.

"We are but we've watched plenty of folks being beat up on the street. The funeral of the police officer was the spark, but things have been getting ugly around here for a while. White folks, especially the Irish, resent us taking jobs they think they should have. I don't doubt the bosses pay us less so they make more profit by hiring us instead. But that ain't our fault, we've all gotta earn a living."

"It seems some things never change," sighed Mosa. "I was here during the riot of 1863. We were burned out of the orphanage back then. I really thought they were gonna kill us. Make sure you stay indoors until things have calmed down."

It was a week later when Thomas turned up unexpectedly at Mosa's apartment.

"What's wrong? Ain't you supposed to be at work?"

"The boss fired me and every other black guy. I bet there's been pressure from City Hall. The Mayor wants to help secure his re-election."

"Oh dear, come on in and I'll fix you something to eat. What will you do?"

"It ain't all bad news. I got an audition with a guy who's formed a band up here in Harlem.

There's over one hundred musicians. He calls it an orchestra, though we don't play classical music. There's even talk of performing at Carnegie Hall and maybe going to Europe on tour. If I get accepted, I'll move the family up here. It feels less threatening than where we live."

"Well, I sure hope you get it. It'd be nice to have you closer."

The night she and Elijah went with Harriet to watch Thomas perform at Carnegie Hall was one of the most happy and memorable occasions of Mosa's life. Taking their place in the plush red seats in the upper balcony, Mosa couldn't help but be impressed by the sheer scale of the venue which accommodated over three thousand.

She'd bought an elegant green dress beaded with imitation emeralds which shone when the lights caught them. Mosa wanted to look her best for her son's special evening. Seeing Thomas come on stage in his tuxedo brought a lump to her throat. After all those nights on the Mississippi and in dubious dives playing for little reward, her boy had finally achieved his dream, a full time job doing what he loved.

"I want to know who my father is." Mosa had been expecting Josephine to ask this question one day but it still took her by surprise.

"He's a man from New Orleans."

"And? You know his name, don't you?" Already thirteen and as tall as her grandmother, Josephine looked her squarely in the eye.

"Émile Dampierre's his name."

"He sounds French. Is that how Mama got to visit Paris?"

"His ancestors came over from France many years ago, and yes, she accompanied his grandmother as her maid when they all went to Paris and that's where you were created."

"Does he know I exist?"

Fearing where telling her the truth might lead, Mosa lied. "Yes, but I'm afraid he wanted nothing to do with you." Josephine's face crumpled. "Come here." Mosa placed her arms around her. The man would doubtless be married with a family. He'd almost certainly reject any approach from Josephine. It was surely better to hurt her now than let her cling to hope, only to see it dashed on the rocks of prejudice and cause an even greater pain.

"In reality then, I'm an orphan like you were. At least I know who my parents are."

Mosa resisted the temptation to comfort her by saying her mother would be coming back one day. To do so seemed unkind. Maisie didn't seem likely to return, and if she did that didn't necessarily mean she would be a proper mother and not cause Josephine more distress than she already had.

Mosa had considered taking Josephine to Paris now she was older but worried it would only cause her heartache. In any event, she and Elijah didn't have the money needed to travel to France.

His business had declined and he'd recently been forced to sell it for a fraction of its worth. The proceeds would let them live out their lives with a roof over their heads but that was about the extent of it. Mosa continued working at the orphanage so she could pay for Josephine to pursue her schooling now she'd reached the age when free education in the city school system had come to an end. If she could, Mosa intended to work for several more years to see her granddaughter through college.

CHAPTER 26

Josephine didn't forget his name. She often imagined how he must look and whether she was similar in appearance. Maybe he'd feel different about her if he knew how pale her skin was. Josephine clung to the possibility that one of her parents might want her. It made her hurt less.

She couldn't remember her mother who'd left when she was so little. At times, Josephine thought about writing to her mother and sometimes she would pen a few lines. But she'd always end up screwing up the paper and throwing it on the fire, frustrated she didn't know the woman who should have been the person in Josephine's life to whom she was closest.

Josephine was seventeen when she decided to do something about finding her father. At least he probably still lived in the United States, unlike her mother.

Dressing in her best outfit, a red and green plaid jacket and a white blouse with layered frills and a green dress, she took the recently opened subway downtown to East Village to visit the Astor

Library. New York's iconic public library next to Bryant Park was then still under construction.

The librarian was an earnest man wearing a monocle. Despite conveying a serious and unwelcoming demeanor, he proved to be most helpful. He recommended Josephine sit at one of the long tables while he went to find the appropriate volume. Others at the table looked up at the new arrival. Josephine felt uncomfortable in the spotlight of their stares, but their curiosity satisfied they buried their heads in their books once more.

The man returned and laid a volume down before her, opened at the correct page. "You can read all about him here."

Her heart fluttering, Josephine read the information. New Orleans based, Émile Dampierre was a well known art dealer, importing paintings and sculptures from Europe with galleries in New Orleans, Chicago, and New York. New York. The two words shouted out at her from the page. Surely that must mean the man visited the city from time to time.

The librarian was happy to oblige a second time in answer to her question. "The gallery is on the corner of Fifth and 53rd."

Riding the subway again, Josephine went to find it. A poster on the window proclaimed an exhibition of the latest art from France. Opening night was only two weeks away. Josephine was swept home on a tide of optimism. He would most likely be there for that. It would be her chance to meet him, at last.

By the time she reached Harlem, her exhilaration had surrendered to fatalism. He didn't want anything to do with her. Even if she managed to get in, what would she say to him? He'd hardly be pleased to have his grand opening ruined by the appearance of the illegitimate daughter he had most probably completely forgotten about.

Mosa stopped fretting about where her granddaughter could possibly be when Thomas burst in, his face radiant with excitement.

"Guess what, I'm going on a tour of Europe."

"That's wonderful."

Thomas must have read her thoughts for he answered the question without her having to ask it. "We're playing in Paris. I'll write to Maisie tonight."

"I do hope you get to see her. It's been over fifteen years since she left. Give her my love and let her know that me and Josephine are always thinking of her. When do you leave?"

"Next month."

"I don't think we should mention you're going to Paris to Josephine, it might upset her."

"If that's what you want."

"Depending how things go with Maisie when you're there, we can decide whether it would be a good idea to tell her on your return."

Josephine kept her discovery to herself. She didn't

feel like talking about it and didn't want the added pressure of her grandmother's concern. If the man refused to speak to her, it would be easier if no one else knew that she'd tried and failed.

On the afternoon of the opening, she pleaded a headache and went to her room and sneaked out when her grandmother and Elijah went for their daily stroll. Pacing up and down outside the gallery, she observed the faces of middle aged men as they passed her. Josephine hoped he'd arrive early to give her a chance to talk to him.

She knew it was him even before it became obvious he was going to enter the building.

"Can I have a moment of your time?"

Émile halted and jerked his head backward. Maybe he, too, saw the similarity.

"Who are you?"

"Josephine, your daughter."

His jaw dropped. "I don't understand."

"Maisie's my mother. I take it you remember her."

The colour fled from his cheeks as if a ghost had walked right through him.

"I'm not here to embarrass you, I only wanted to meet you."

Émile looked around furtively, doubtless concerned someone he knew might see them. "Let's go in the hotel next door, they have a cafe."

"Forgive me if I seem surprised," he said once they were seated in a corner in the back of the room. "I never knew. My grandmother said she'd caught your mother trying to steal something and had fired her. I can see now that wasn't so, and she must have known about you. I can definitely see me in you but I'm surprised you're...How can I put this..."

"So white?"

"Yes."

"Believe me, I often wonder the same thing."

"Is your mother in New York?"

"No, she lives in Paris. I live up in Harlem with my grandmother. She raised me."

Émile leaned forward and lowered his voice to almost a whisper. "What is it you want of me? I'm a married man with a family."

Josephine maintained her composure even though inside she was in turmoil. There was no joy in his face at meeting his daughter for the first time, and no thought for what she'd endured, only concern for himself that she might damage his reputation.

"I wanted to meet you, that's all. Anyway, I mustn't keep you. Goodbye." She quickly stood up to leave so she could turn her back on him and he wouldn't see her pain which was fast becoming uncontainable.

"Wait." Josephine halted. "Can you meet at the Waldorf tomorrow, for lunch?"

She nodded, not wanting her voice to betray her emotion and quickly hurried from the room.

When she arrived home, Mosa was in her rocking chair, knitting.

"Where've you been?"

"Walking around Central Park." Josephine felt no guilt in lying. After all, it seemed clear her grandmother had lied in telling her that her father wanted nothing to do with her. She believed his explanation. The way he'd looked, the shock on his face. Josephine was as certain as she could be that he hadn't known she existed.

"Well, you're sure dressed up for a walk, wearing your very best outfit. Are you courting somebody?"

"No, I'm not," said Josephine hoping the sudden rush of heat she was experiencing wasn't reflected on her face. "There's nothing wrong with a young woman wanting to look pretty."

"I guess there ain't." But her grandmother's tone indicated she remained suspicious.

CHAPTER 27

Josephine held out her hands in front of her as she entered the Waldorf and looked down at them. She hadn't expected them to be as steady as they were. The anxiety of yesterday had passed. She'd met her father but, contrary to her expectation, she harbored no sense of loss. All those years of not knowing him no longer mattered the way they once had. In short, there was no bond between them, only a biological one which exerted no pull. Josephine wasn't sure why she'd even come. She thought about leaving but he'd already spotted her. He stood up from the table and offered a smile she didn't believe was entirely sincere.

"How was opening night?" asked Josephine.

"It went very well."

They exchanged pleasantries while they examined the menu. When their lobster bisque arrived, Émile became personal.

"You're very beautiful, like your mother."

Josephine didn't want flattery and his remark annoyed her, emboldening her to speak her mind in a forthright manner. "She was also very young. What exactly was your plan? Clearly no upstanding gentleman from New Orleans would intend to marry somebody of her color."

"Maybe not, but something wonderful came out of it, you."

Josephine's cheeks flamed. "Oh, please. You abused your position of power against an innocent young woman. You took advantage of her with no regard for the consequences she, but not you, would suffer."

"I'd like to make amends. How much do you need?" From his jacket, he pulled out his checkbook and opened it, pen poised.

Josephine pushed back her chair and stood up. "Nothing, I don't want your money. You didn't care what happened to my mother all those years ago so don't pretend you care now about me. I need to go."

Josephine pushed her shoulders back as she walked home. She'd had her answer. He thought he could buy her off but he couldn't. She refused to let the encounter weaken her. She'd already had plenty of knocks in life to cope with yet one more.

Josephine was proud she had spoken up and challenged her father. He probably wasn't in the least bothered about what she said and his ordered and 'respectable' life wouldn't miss a beat.

Yet something positive had come from their meeting. It had given her closure.

She would make her own way in this world, exactly as her grandmother and mother had done. Mosa would be her role model, not him. Her father might be rich but that didn't make a person kind or admirable.

"Non," replied the stoney-faced man at the front desk with the infamous hauteur of a Parisian hotelier, accompanied by a shrug of the shoulders when Thomas asked. He sloped away, dispirited.

Within Thomas, sadness and anger fought for dominance. Berlin and London had been exciting. The European audiences went wild for their music. All seemed set fair for their last stop on the tour. Paris was to have been the highlight, a family reunion after so much time apart. He didn't understand how Maisie could behave like this, and especially with him, the elder brother she'd once followed around and idolized.

"Why are you looking so glum? We're in Paris, you've gotta have some fun," said one of his bandmates when they passed in the corridor.

"Family troubles."

"Come out with me tonight, a bunch of us are going to the Folies Bergères after our performance this evening. It's supposed to be a great club. You'll be able to forget about your worries for a while." Thomas hesitated. "Come on man, you owe it to yourself after all the work we've put in these last few weeks."

The atmosphere was both intimate and lively, men mainly, come to see the dancing girls of Paris. Thomas forgot his disappointment while he watched them dance the energetic 'Can-Can', kicking their legs high in the air and showing their undergarments. Soon he was laughing and grinning from ear to ear like his friends, thoughts of Maisie forgotten. The women exited to huge applause.

The stage went dark. The tropical beat of bongo drums filled the anticipatory silence. A spotlight illuminated a solitary African woman, barefoot with a short skirt, and on her head an extravagant headdress of yellow feathers fanning out like a sunflower. Her upper half was naked, save for many rows of pearl necklaces which hid her breasts.

She gyrated and spun, her head up, down, sideways. Her movements were so fast it was impossible to discern her facial features. The effect mesmerized the audience who were completely entranced by the spectacle.

Like 'La Danse Bohème' in Bizet's Carmen, the music became faster and faster and the woman danced ever more quickly, falling to the floor at the end in a dramatic climax. The entire theatre leaped to their feet in a thunderous ovation.

The dancer rose to bow. She looked out at a sea of faces and smiled in response to their deafening shouts for more. One man ran onto the stage to present her with a bouquet of roses and stole a kiss on the cheek. She stood there proud and assured, the queen of all she surveyed, an African empress.

Thomas's mouth became dry and his Adam's apple went up then down as he swallowed hard.

He'd never expected it to be her. So glamorous, so poised, so confident, so unlike the sister he remembered.

The rest of the evening's show passed in a haze. When the final curtain fell, he made his excuses and found his way backstage, causing shrieks of surprise when he opened a door to find the Can-Can dancers in various stages of undress. Making his apologies, he knocked on another door and cautiously opened it.

A woman in a red silk robe sitting at a dressing table saw his reflection in the mirror and turned on her stool. She had never seen her brother in a tuxedo before but she recognized him immediately, her eyes widening at this unexpected visitor.

"Did you get my letter?" She nodded. "Then why didn't you leave a message for me at the hotel."

"Because I knew you'd be judging me, and trying to persuade me to return."

"Well, you do have a seventeen year old daughter you haven't seen since she was knee high to a grasshopper, and a mother approaching seventy who might not have many years left on this earth. Why do you want to cut yourself off from your family? Family still loves you when nobody else does."

Maisie's eyes became rheumy for a moment before she shut the door to her feelings. "If I came back I'd only be opening old wounds and cause hurt by leaving again. My life is here, it's where I belong.

Can't you see how it is? There's so much more freedom than back home. In Paris, you don't need to be white to succeed. I'm adored, worshipped even. You saw how the crowd reacted."

"But what is success with nobody to share it with?"

A knock on the door interrupted their conversation.

"Entrez," called Maisie.

The man wore a black cape draped over his tuxedo. He removed his tall black hat with a flourish. His chestnut hair, deep brown eyes, and aquiline nose confirmed his French heritage.

"This is Pierre. Pierre, this is Thomas, my brother."

"Monsieur." The man inclined his head toward Thomas.

"He doesn't speak much English. We've been together for a few years now. We're going out to eat. Do you want to join us?"

The resentment within Thomas surfaced. "I've already eaten," he lied. "I need to get back to the hotel."

Thomas berated himself while he walked back to his hotel. Why on earth had he behaved like that, throwing away the chance to spend time with his sister? A sister he most likely would never see again.

He raced back to the theatre but the couple had already left. The few people still back stage didn't know where.

Thomas wandered the cobbled streets and peered through restaurant windows, receiving glares of rebuke from those whose privacy he was invading. He gave up and walked to the hotel.

The next evening Thomas went back to the Folies Bergères. He waited outside her dressing room but Maisie didn't appear. He eventually found a dancer who spoke English.

"She's got the week off and taken the train to Nice, lucky thing. She'll soon be strolling by the Mediterranean, arm in arm with that handsome beau of hers. Still, I'm not surprised he's smitten. She's so elegant. She has that 'je ne sais quoi'. All the girls would love to be her."

Thomas cursed inwardly, he'd be gone by the time Maisie returned to Paris.

CHAPTER 28

Thomas could tell from how rigidly his mother held herself that she was upset, even though outwardly she remained calm.

"It's good to know she's not alone. But let's not speak of it to Josephine."

"Don't you think she should know?"

"What good would it do? I want to protect her from being hurt."

"You can't protect her forever."

"Maybe not but I'll do so for as long as I can."

"And how's that helping her?"

"You've no idea what it's like to live without a mother's love. To tell her about her mom's life, the glitz and the glamor, and that she has a partner who she gives her attention to but that she can't be bothered to write to her own daughter, would crush her more than she is already."

Josephine also made plans for a secret of her own.

"I've got a job as a waitress," she announced to her grandmother while she helped prepare dinner.

"A waitress?" repeated Mosa, putting down the knife she was using to peel the potatoes.

"Whatever for? The plan was for you to become a teacher."

"That was your plan, grandma. I appreciate all you've done for me, I really do, but I intend becoming a secretary. I want to work in an office with adults, not a room full of kids. My wages from working evenings as a waitress will pay for it."

"Well, if that's what you want," harrumphed Mosa.

"It is. You should keep the money you've saved, not spend it on me. You've worked hard your whole life. It's time for you to relax and enjoy yourself. You and Elijah could take a trip, go to Paris maybe."

One morning a few weeks later, Josephine left the house with a spring in her step. Rounding the corner, she removed a wig from her bag to hide her tight curls and placed it on her head.

Josephine's confidence deserted her the moment she arrived. Her eyes darted around the room when she entered, a room full of young women, each of them white, genuinely white. They weren't pretending like she was.

Josephine feared they'd all turn and stare and ask what she thought she was doing here, that they'd immediately know she wasn't who she appeared to be. But no one did. Some gave her a smile.

She sat down at one of the desks in the last row, it felt safer there behind others and out of sight. Moments later the teacher came in. "Good morning, ladies. Let's start by introducing ourselves. I'm Miss Brown. Now starting from the

THE ANSWER'S LOVE

back, I want you to stand in turn and introduce yourself."

Josephine gulped, she would be first. She stood but no words would come.

"Yes?"

Josephine wanted to become invisible. "Jo... Josephine Elwood." Her nervousness would surely expose her.

"Next."

Josephine relaxed, a little.

She tensed once again when two young women approached her at the end of the lesson. Their eyes seemed to be probing her as if they suspected.

"I'm Rose and this is Nancy. We're going to get a coffee. Did you want to join us?"

Josephine agreed. If she was going to try passing she'd need to get used to mixing with white folks. Even so her mouth had become as parched as the Sahara.

"Did you see that?" said Rose after the waitress took their order. "A colored girl serving us. Whatever next? They'll be trying to attend our college before you know it."

"My father says there's hundreds of them arriving in the city every single day, coming up from the South. They ought to stay there, where they belong," said Nancy.

"I agree," said Rose. "What do you think, Josephine?"

"I guess. I've never really thought about it."

"Well you should. The Civil War was fought to end

slavery, not to let them take over. So tell us, where are your family from?"

"My father was born here but my mother came from Spain."

"I thought so, that's what I said to Nancy. That your family must be from somewhere like that. You have that Mediterranean look, a slightly darker skin tone and those ebony eyes. Though don't get me wrong, we think you're beautiful."

Josephine blushed.

That evening Josephine reflected on her first day of deception. It was easier than she thought. Her skin color allowed her to pass with ease. She had to lie about her family but after the first time she did so with ease.

When Josephine passed the examination, she found a position in a bank on Wall Street and a room to rent near to her work. Josephine loved wandering the busy streets of New York. There was a palpable energy to downtown. An affirmation of life, a life without barriers, and she was finally living it.

With her spare money, Josephine bought fashionable new clothes. They made her feel good and feel like she belonged. No longer was she uncomfortable in her own skin, and her parents' rejection of her no longer defined who she was. Josephine had never experienced such an exhilarating rush of contentment and freedom.

The bank hummed with the clatter of typewriters

and hormones. Many young people worked there, all white of course and predominantly male.

One young man in particular caught her attention with his fair hair and blue eyes, his chiseled jawline, and confident gait. Over time his smiles when he passed her desk became words, if only short greetings limited to 'how are you' and introducing himself as Erik.

Josephine had been at the bank for a few months when he asked her out. He took her to a trattoria in Little Italy where they dined by candlelight. Josephine wore a pale pink lace like dress with a rounded neck line. She could sense from the lustre in his eyes that Erik was smitten.

"Tell me about your family."

Josephine repeated the story she'd already given to others who had asked. "I don't have one. My parents passed a few years back and I don't have any siblings "

Josephine was already accomplished at being someone she wasn't.

Josephine's plans for a double life had become a reality. She lived in two worlds, moving effortlessly between them. She visited Mosa and Elijah in Harlem every other weekend but didn't mention her beau.

Her grandmother would never understand, how could she? No one would mistake her for being white. Josephine didn't know how else she was supposed to live in a society where the color of skin was more important than the person who inhabited it.

If Josephine were to marry a black man, people would assume it was a mixed race marriage. At best, they'd be looked down upon. More than likely they'd face intimidation and violence, especially her husband. It wasn't a path she wished to go down. Why face a lifetime of animosity and rejection when she didn't need to, she reasoned.

After that first dinner, the young couple saw each other outside work every weekend. Holding hands progressed to passionate kissing in alleyways.

When Erik took her on a walk around Central Park, Josephine complained of sore feet before they reached the northern end by Harlem. Mosa and Elijah regularly took walks in that area, Elijah leaning on his walking stick and Mosa holding him by his arm.

While they took the subway back, Erik asked her to accompany him the following weekend to Brooklyn to meet his parents. "They emigrated from Denmark before I was born. I hope you'll like them."

Josephine stayed awake late that night. Things were becoming serious. She really liked Erik. He was decisive and protective.

There'd never been a strong male presence in her life. Elijah had always treated her well but he'd been out working most of the time she was growing up. She struggled to keep a conversation with him going when her grandmother wasn't around. They had nothing in common, apart from a love for Mosa.

A love for Mosa. Josephine swallowed. She didn't want to cause her grief like her mother had. Her grandmother had always been there for her. She didn't deserve such treatment, yet Josephine couldn't see any way to avoid it. She'd still visit her grandmother but she could never introduce Erik to her. He could never know she existed.

That Sunday, Josephine went up to Harlem to see her grandmother. Elijah was dozing in his chair which he did a great deal of these days, head bowed and dribble leaking from the corner of his mouth. Josephine suggested they go for a stroll in nearby Morningside Park.

It was a fine May day, the trees a luscious green. Their leaves created a pleasing dappled sunlight. Josephine clenched her fists, preparing for a conversation she didn't want to have.

"Let's sit down on this bench, I've got something I want to tell you." Her grandmother raised her eyebrows and threw her a quizzical look. "I've met somebody and I think he might be going to ask me to marry him." The words spilled more quickly from her than she'd intended.

Mosa placed her hand on Josephine's arm. "The real question is do you want to marry him? You're only eighteen, that's still young."

"Yes, I believe I do."

"But your dilemma is he's white."

Josephine was flabbergasted. "How did you know?"
"It doesn't take a genius. You're working downtown at a bank where I don't suppose they hire our kind, and I know you've never felt at home in our world. I always expected you might try passing when you grew up. After all, no one would know the truth if they didn't meet your relatives. I can't blame you, life is easier for white people in so many ways. I'm guessing he doesn't know about me or your mother." Josephine hung her head and fiddled with her fingers. "Well? Are you gonna answer me?"
"No, he doesn't. I worry he wouldn't want me if he did. That's my problem. I don't want to hurt you but what am I to do? How else can I live? Being stuck between black and white is so hard."
"I was going to marry a white man once, here in New York, but he went off to fight in the Civil War and it never happened." Josephine's mouth opened in amazement. "Of course, he could see my true color or thought he could."
Josephine's brow furrowed. "Thought he could? What do you mean?'
"My parents were white."
"White? I don't understand. Everyone can see from your skin tone that you probably had a white father, but surely you're not saying your mother was white too? And… wait a minute, you've always told me you were an orphan and didn't know who your parents were."
"I know, it's a secret I've shared with very few. I

probably should have told you sooner but I didn't think it would help you to know. I realize now that was probably wrong of me. My color is a throwback to an African ancestor on my father's side of the family so I understand how difficult it is when you feel you don't belong in your own skin. My parents didn't want me. My father wanted me drowned the day I was born. He ordered a brave and wonderful woman, a slave named Maisie and who I named your mother after, to throw me in the river. But she saved me and I was brought up as a slave."

Josephine placed a hand over her mouth, still astonished by her grandmother's revelations. Mosa continued, "All I've ever wanted for you is for you to be happy, and I don't want you worrying about me." Tears pricked Josephine's eyes. Her grandmother had always been such a giving person, never asking for anything in return. "But if you love someone there should be no secrets between you, especially one this big. The truth has a way of making itself known whether you like it or not. If you have a baby, the child may not be as white as you are. Color is definitely a variable in our family."

"I'd take care of it," said Josephine.

"That's easy to say now. It won't be so easy when you find out you're pregnant. To deny yourself the joy of children is something you'll likely bitterly regret in a few years. And what about him? Is it right to deny him a child if he wants one?" Josephine didn't respond. "I'll say no more. I'll leave you now, you've a lot to think about."

Mosa bent forward as she stood and kissed Josephine's forehead. "Remember, I love you and will support you whatever you decide."

"I'm so lucky to have you, grandma."

"And me you. One thing I've learned in my long life is the answer to our problems, to the world's problems, is love. Only love can conquer hatred. And one day I hope it will, and then what color a person is won't matter no more."

CHAPTER 29

Josephine remained, deep in thought. Even when raindrops fell in their millions and turned the park into a watercolor of blurred lines and smudges she stayed, a solitary figure. Not until her wet clothes clung to her like a leech did she head for the subway.

Her grandmother was right, living a lie was no way to live. If Erik truly loved her, he'd accept her for who she was. She must tell him before they visited his parents. She needed to know.

Not wanting her colleagues to notice, Josephine waited until Erik walked passed her desk as he headed for the restrooms. She followed and softly called out his name when they were both out of sight of the other employees.

"I thought we'd agreed not to talk at work so people wouldn't know about us," said Erik, a strong hiss of rebuke in his voice.

"We did but I have to speak to you before we visit your parents this weekend. Can you meet me down at Battery Park after work. There's something I need to ask you."

Josephine got there first and sat on a bench overlooking the water and out toward the Statue of Liberty, that symbol of societal perfection which didn't exist in the real world A chilly wind was blowing and Josephine sunk her head into her jacket and raised her collar for warmth.

"So, what is it?" demanded Erik the moment he arrived.

"I need to know if you truly want me for who I am or for only who you think I am."

Erik's forehead creased in confusion. "I don't understand. Aren't you who you say you are?"

"Yes, I'm Josephine Elwood but I'm not the orphan I said I was. My mother lives in Paris and my father in New Orleans. I'm the result of their brief affair. I don't see either of them. My grandmother, who lives in New York, raised me."

"Are you saying you're illegitimate? That doesn't bother me but my parents are old school so we best not mention it to them."

"There's more." Josephine raised her hand to her head and removed her wig to reveal tight black curls. "My mother's black."

Erik shot to his feet. "Black! You've gotta be kidding me." Josephine shook her head. "So you tricked me into loving you. I was gonna ask you to marry me but this changes everything." He spat his words out in anger. "I could never marry a nigger, never. It'd ruin my career. I can't believe how you've lied. I don't ever want to see you again." He stormed off but halted and turned after only a few steps.

"And you need to resign first thing tomorrow or I'll tell your boss exactly who you are, and then you'll never get a reference."

Mosa could tell the instant her granddaughter walked in from the dark circles under her eyes and lacklustre expression. Josephine sank into her grandmother's open arms. That same refuge of warmth and softness which had made Josephine feel better as a child whenever something bad happened to her.

"How about you move back in here and let me take care of you while you work out what you'll do now," said Mosa.

"Thank you, but no. I'm gonna be strong, like you. I'll find a new job and move on. Life knocked you down plenty of times but each and every time you got back up. I've got to learn to do the same."

That evening Mosa wrote a letter. When the reply came it wasn't evasive like she thought it would be, although the letter was almost as short as her previous ones.

I think your idea is great and so does Pierre, my husband.
I'd so love to see you, but Pierre insists we won't visit a country where we can't both stay in the same hotel room or eat in the same restaurant. You know you and Elijah would always be welcome here. You could stay as long as you like, for always if you wanted to.
I've given up the dancing Thomas will have told you about. I'm getting too old for it! Since I married

Pierre I only did it for the enjoyment. He has a good inheritance and there's no need for me to work.

When Josephine visited her grandmother's, Mosa waited until after lunch and until Elijah was snoring in his chair.

"I've had a letter from your mother. I wrote to her about you."

"I don't understand."

"When she came back from Paris pregnant with you, she tried to persuade me to move to Paris with her. She said we'd be truly free there, that our color wouldn't hold us back. I refused to go and leave Thomas and his family so she went alone. She's written to you too."

Josephine took the letter and placed it on the table when her shaking hands made it difficult to read.

My dear Josephine,
I'm so sorry to hear of your troubles. I realize it can't be easy looking white when your family are black, not in America at least.

I came to Paris because I disliked how my color limited me. I needed to escape the restrictions imposed on me in the States.

Here, my color has never held me back. I think you too would find France liberating, and that if you fell in love your ancestry would be unlikely to be a problem. My husband, Pierre, is white and that's never been an issue. The Parisians are content to live and let live.

I know I haven't been a good mother, not even a mother at all. I'd hoped that you and your grandmother would one day move here but that's no excuse. I put myself first by coming to Paris, unlike your grandmother who has always put others before herself.

I would so welcome the opportunity to have you come live here with us. We have no financial worries, and should you decide it's not for you, we'll buy you a ticket back to New York.

If you decide to come, I'll wire you the money for your outward bound crossing.

"There's no need to make a decision yet," said Mosa. "Think about it."

"But what about you?"

Mosa laid her hands on Josephine's. "Your mother invited Elijah and me too but I don't want to leave my home. Maybe if I was younger but I've spent too much of my life going from place to place. I'm done with all that. The two of us will be just fine. Thomas and Harriet are only a couple of blocks away if we need anything. Now is your time, and whatever you decide you want mustn't be limited by worrying about me. And I'd love for you to form a relationship with your mother. I won't be around for ever, and I hate to think of you being without a mother to fall back on when times are tough."

Josephine flung her arms around her. "Oh, Grandma you're the nicest person I know. Everything I am and can be is because of you."

"I've decided to go to Paris and give it a try, though I'll miss you terribly," said Josephine the next time she visited.

"And me you, but I'm glad you and your mother will be reunited. It'll be an exciting adventure, and an opportunity to live the life you deserve."

Josephine produced a large notebook from her bag. "Before I go, there's something I want to do. I want you to tell me all about your life. All that you've gone through and the wonderful things you've done should never be forgotten. With your permission, I'd like to write a book about you."

"Me? I doubt anyone would want to read about me."

"On the contrary, they most certainly will. Your story will be an inspiration to so many."

Mosa doubted that but she indulged her granddaughter and wandered the avenues of her past to satisfy Josephine. Over the next few weeks, Josephine filled three notebooks while her grandmother reminisced, sometimes laughing at a memory and sometimes wiping a tear from her eyes as she recalled the injustices and those who'd been killed for trying to make the world a better place.

Josephine only hoped she could do justice to this remarkable woman.

On the day of Josephine's departure, Mosa and Elijah accompanied her to the boat. Their conversation was superficial. Both grandmother and granddaughter feared setting off uncontrollable emotion if they said what they were really feeling. The hug goodbye was brief. Josephine ascended the gangway without once turning, not wanting her grandmother to see her upset.

Elijah took a handkerchief from his jacket pocket and gave it to Mosa.

"Thank you," she said, dabbing her eyes. "I'm happy for her, it's only right she pursues her own path."

Elijah put his arm around her shoulder. "It is but that don't make it any easier for you."

"She wasn't mine to keep. I've been blessed to have so many years with her. And look how lucky I am. I have you, and Thomas and his family. He told me yesterday Nate and his wife are expecting a child so I'll soon be a great grandmother.

"Those times when it seemed like I would have money and an easy life and then lost it all I felt sad, cheated even. I used to wonder why me. But it was a good lesson. It taught me it's people, not money or things, which bring happiness. Love's the most important thing, nothing else really matters."

CHAPTER 30

"Sit down and relax, woman," said Elijah. "You've been up cleaning since six this morning and the place ain't even dirty."

Mosa put down her dust cloth and gratefully sank into an armchair. Her back ached and she was already weary. She looked at the clock for the umpteenth time. They'd be here any moment now. Years of separation were down to minutes, maybe only seconds.

When they knocked at the door she started and then eased herself out of the chair as quickly as her old body would allow her.

"Mama!" Mother and daughter embraced, crying with both joy and sadness. Sadness for so many years passed without seeing each other but joyful they were once again reunited. Josephine and Elijah smiled and blinked back tears while they watched the mother and child reunion.

"My dear child," said Mosa stepping back to get a good look at her daughter. Maisie looked every bit the striking Parisian in her ruffled blouse and long green coat and a matching hat with a large feather.

"I've missed you so much." Mosa hugged her again tightly for confirmation she wasn't dreaming.

So many times Mosa had yearned for this precious moment. Until a telegram arrived last week, she was reconciled to dying without seeing her daughter one last time.

"Me too, Mama. Me too."

"And Josephine, you look more radiant than ever. Life in France must be suiting you."

"It does, Grandma, but it's so wonderful to see you again."

"Sit yourselves down while I make you both some coffee."

"No need, let me take us all out for lunch," said Maisie.

Elijah made his excuses. He couldn't walk more than a few steps these days and didn't enjoy social gatherings. With his increasing deafness, all he would hear would be the mangled din of a conversation.

The three generations of Elwood women went to a nearby restaurant with huge potted plants and big windows that let in the spring sunshine.

"Isn't this nice," said Mosa.

"It is, though in Paris we'd be free to eat in any restaurant we wanted to and sit amongst white folks," said Maisie.

Mosa didn't care about that, not today, and changed the subject. "So, Josephine, tell me, do you like Paris?"

"It's all I hoped it would be and more, and being

with Mama makes it all the better."

"I'm glad. And what have you been doing? Do you have a job? You never mentioned working in your letters."

Josephine glanced at her mother who gave her daughter a conspiratorial nod. "We've something for you." She leaned to one side and pulled a book from the bag which she'd placed on the floor next to her and passed it to her grandmother.

Mosa moved an index finger over the gold-colored letters indented on the plain blue cover, reading the title as she did so, 'One woman's struggle to be free'.

"We wrote it, it's all about you."

Mosa was temporarily dumbfounded. Her life in this book, the story of all the good and the bad, and of those she had loved and lost. A wave of emotion hit Mosa but she refused to cry. Today was a wonderful occasion, a time for happiness and gratitude, not sadness or regret. "Oh my... I don't know what to say."

"It's a literary sensation in both France and Britain," explained her granddaughter.

"Sadly, it's not here. Not yet anyway," added Maisie. "Our publisher in Europe has been in touch with all the major publishing houses in New York. They say it wouldn't appeal to their readers but we're not giving up, and while we're here we'll be knocking on every door. The royalties from sales in Europe are already significant. I'll write you a check for them. After all, it's your story, not ours."

"I don't need money at my age. Keep half for you both and split that with Thomas. I'd like to donate the other half to the Colored Orphanage."

Mosa reached her hands across the table toward the other two. They each took one of her wrinkled hands, hands which had labored so hard and for so long but also hands which had communicated so much love and comfort.

"I'm truly blessed and immensely proud of both of you. Thank you, thank you so much."

"I'm sorry I hurt you by leaving," said Maisie.

"You did what you felt you needed to do. I don't want to dwell on the past, life is too short for that. You're here now so let's enjoy our time together. All I wanted for you, for all my family, was for you all to be happy. I can see you and Josephine have formed a strong bond and that brings me great joy. Everything is good in my world. It may have taken a lifetime but I got there. Now, let's eat, I'm hungry."

++++++++++++++++++++++++++

ALSO BY DAVID CANFORD

Bound Bayou

A young teacher from England achieves a dream when he gets the chance to work for a year in the United States, but 1950s Mississippi is not the America he has seen on the movie screens at home. When his independent spirit collides with the rules of life in the Deep South, he sets off a chain of events he can't control.

The Shadows of Seville

A gripping and moving story of loss and love, of hatred and passion, and of horror and hope, set in Spain's most evocative city during the turmoil of the Spanish Civil War and the following decades. Lose yourself in vibrant 'Sevilla' where the shadows of the past are around every corner.

Puppets of Prague

Can the dream of freedom overcome fear and oppression? Friendships are tested to the limit in this saga spanning Prague's tumultuous 20th century. In the summer of 1914 young love beckons and the future seems bright for three close friends, but momentous events throw into stark relief the differences between them that had never mattered before.

Betrayal in Venice

Sent to Venice on a secret mission against the Nazis, a soldier finds his life unexpectedly altered when he saves a young woman at the end of World War Two. Discovering the truth many years later, Glen Butler's reaction to it betrays the one he loves most.

A Good Nazi? The Lies We Keep

Growing up in 1930s Germany two boys, one

Catholic and one Jewish, become close friends. After Hitler seizes power, their lives are changed forever. When World War 2 comes, will they help each other, or will secrets from their teenage years make them enemies?

Kurt's War

Kurt is an English evacuee with a difference. His father is a Nazi. As Kurt grows into an adult and is forced to pretend that he is someone he isn't for his own protection, will he survive in the hostile world in which he must live? And with his enemies closing in, will even the woman he loves believe who he really is?

A Heart Left Behind

New Yorker, Orla, finds herself trapped in a web of secret love, blackmail and espionage in the build up to WW2. Moving to Berlin and hoping to escape her past, she is forced to undertake a task that will cost not only her own life but also that of her son if she fails.

Going Big or Small

British humour collides with European culture in this tale of 'it's never too late'. Retiree, Frank, gets more adventure than he bargained for when he sets off across 1980s Europe hoping to shake up his mundane life. Falling in love with a woman and Italy has unexpected consequences.

Sea Snakes and Cannibals

A travelogue of visits to islands around the world, including remote Fijian islands, Corsica, islands in the Sea of Cortez, Mexico, and the Greek islands.

When the Water Runs Out

Will water shortage result in the USA invading Canada? One person can stop a war if he isn't killed first but is he a hero or a traitor? When two very different worlds collide, the outcome is on a knife-edge.

2045 The Last Resort

In 2045 those who lost their jobs to robots are taken care of in resorts where life is an endless vacation. For those still in work, the American dream has never been better. But is all quite as perfect as it seems?

THANK YOU

I hope you enjoyed reading 'The Answer's Love'. I would appreciate it if you could spare a few moments to post a review on Amazon. It only need be a few words.

Thanks so much,

David Canford

ABOUT THE AUTHOR

Writing historical fiction, David Canford is able to combine his love of history and travel in novels that take readers on a rollercoaster journey through time and place with characters who face struggle and hardship but where resilience, love and forgiveness can overcome hatred and oppression.

He has also written two novels about the future, and a travelogue.

David has three grown up daughters and lives on the south coast of England with his wife and their dog.

You can contact him via his Facebook page or at David.Canford@hotmail.com

Printed in Great Britain
by Amazon